CROAKIES DICTUM

SAM CHEEVER

ELECTRIC PROSE PUBLICATIONS

~

Sometimes the only decision you can make is the wrong one. Then, all you can hope for is that two wrongs DO make a right. Also, don't mess with Dave.

Someone has taken fairy Queen Sindra and all the fae and locked them away. For their safe return, the villain is demanding the most powerful artifact in existence. Unfortunately, the artifact is in the protective custody of The Universe, which is the main governing body for all magic. It's being protected by a powerful magician, a three-headed anti-mythological feline, and a guy named Dave.

Don't ask me about the Dave thing. I don't have a clue.

The only way we can save the entire fae population is to get our hands on that artifact. Our journey promises to be epic. Alas, it doesn't promise to be successful.

Any way I look at it, things stand a really good chance of going horribly, epically wrong. Good thing I'm used to things going hideously wrong. In fact, it's become something of a signature move for me.

STAY IN TOUCH

Sam doesn't give away a lot of books. But she values her readers and, to show it, she's gifting you a copy of a fun book just for signing up for her newsletter!

SIGN UP HERE!
https://samcheever.com/newsletter/

1

YOU'RE USING YOUR KINDLY VOICE?
ON ME?

All around me were green, growing things. The sweet scents of pears and apples warred with the floral scents of dozens of flowering plants and the verdant richness of herbs. A thousand colors bloomed around me, and a few hundred whirring wings formed a pleasant backdrop to the sights and smells, providing the auditory component the scene needed to achieve perfection.

My best friend Lea's enormous back-lot greenhouse was my second favorite place to be. Second only to the magical artifact library and bookstore I called home.

My errand in the greenhouse, however, was not my favorite thing. In fact, for the tenth or thousandth time...I wasn't sure which but it seemed like a lot...I mentally cursed my assistant and, yes, friend Sebille's insistence that I try to convince her mother to stay in Enchanted.

Convincing the queen of the fairies in Enchanted to do anything she didn't want to do was a nearly impossible task. I had a newfound understanding of Sebille's obstinance.

It was clearly in her DNA.

"But the plants need you," I tried again. The focus of my

pleading buzzed from lavender bush to monkshood plant to rosemary shrub, sprinkling fairy dust over one and all.

Queen Sindra wore a rare glower on her tiny, beautiful face, her movements more rigidly energetic than was customary for the laid-back ruler. Her vibrant pink, purple, and neon green butterfly wings whirred with abnormal verve as she attempted to show me how irritating I was being.

In pure desperation, I held out the tiny, sickly plant Sebille had shoved into my hands before I'd come. "Look. This is just one of hundreds of plants Lea received from the grower this week. The man is clearly a charlatan."

Sindra's green eyes, so like her daughter's, skimmed reluctantly toward the plant and a hungry look slipped across her face before she squelched it. Seeing my opening, I renewed my efforts.

"We were really counting on you and the fairies to heal and encourage them. It will take weeks. Maybe longer," I told her. "Maybe after that we can talk about why you want to leave."

Hands on hips, Sindra stamped a tiny foot on the air.

I blinked. I'd never seen the queen so angry. Swallowing hard, I had to admit to myself that her anger was focused on me.

I didn't think Queen Sindra had ever been mad at *me*. I didn't like it one bit.

"I do not discuss my decisions with magical librarians or kind but interfering earth witches, or..." Her gaze took on a glint that didn't bode well for the next person on her list. "...bossy daughters who reject our ways and refuse to follow their mother's laws. I am Sindra, queen of the fairies. My decisions are my own to make. And I've decided we need to move to the Primordial Forest. That is the end of that." Her eyes sparked vivid green before she spun in the air and shot away.

"I'm sorry," I called after her. "We love you and will miss you. That's all."

She hesitated, easing to a stop, and then turned back. Her expression softened, and so did the stiff frame of her shoulders. She opened her mouth to respond and hope lit in my chest.

But it was not to be.

The greenhouse shook violently around us.

Fairies throughout the large structure shot upward, their bodies braced and their gazes alert.

Blood pulsed in my ears, a growing pressure making my eardrums ache.

A beat later, the air imploded, leaving me gasping and breathless. I fought to fill my lungs but no air would come.

Then the pressure released with a whoosh and blasted outward, exploding the plexiglass and metal walls of the large building and blowing away its doors.

I was thrown backward, slamming into the hard earth outside the greenhouse. Pain shot through my back and legs as I skidded across the stony soil.

As quickly as it had shifted, the air stilled. Not so much as a wisp of smoke or dust moved through the space.

I lay there gasping for a moment and then crawled to my feet, moving slowly as I scraped my aching body off the ground. I stumbled into the building, terrified of what I'd find.

It was worse than I'd feared.

The area was bathed in silence. Not a single fairy wing whirred in the air. Thank the goddess I saw no bodies littering the ravaged ground. I closed my eyes in relief and sucked in a deep breath, releasing it slowly. But my relief was short lived. The blast might not have killed the fairies. But it had certainly done something.

Queen Sindra and her fairies were all...

Gone?

Shoving my shoulder-length brown hair out of my face, I stumbled through the brutalized building, my horrified blue gaze taking in the complete devastation.

Plants were uprooted and torn. Fruit trees were ripped from the ground, their battered fruit scattered from one end of the structure to the other. The metal sides of the building were torn and twisted. And the little pond in the back had been nearly emptied of water, its rocky waterfall blown away and embedded in the walls.

I was both surprised and pleased to see that Wally, Lea's pet bullfrog was alive and well.

"Bawump!" Wally said in an outraged belch.

"I hear ya, buddy," I told him. "This is not good."

A distant door slammed and Lea screamed my name from the back of her herbal shop. I hurried over and stuck my head through the ravaged door. "I'm okay. Wally's okay too."

Relief filled her pretty face for a beat, then turned to horror as she took in the condition of her wonderful greenhouse. "What happened?"

I shook my head. "I wish I knew. One minute I was talking to Sindra and the next..." Words suddenly failed me. Tears filled my eyes and I swallowed a knot in my throat.

They were all gone.

"Naida?"

I shook my head, a shaky hand covering my mouth. How was I going to tell Sebille?

Lea touched my arm, her hand soft and warm against my icy flesh.

"Where are the fairies?" Lea asked in a terrified whisper.

I turned my tear-drenched gaze her way, not bothering to hide my own horror at the situation.

Lea gasped, tears overflowing her turquoise gaze. She ran fingers through her long, curly, light brown hair, her lips quivering. "It can't be."

I sniffed and pulled her into a hug. At five feet nine inches, I was several inches taller than Lea. She had such a large personality, I rarely thought about it. But she felt small curled against me sobbing, my natural instinct to soothe and protect kicked in.

I smoothed her hair off her face. "They have to be okay," I said. "There's no sign..." I swallowed a lump in my throat, not wanting to say the words. "There has to be some other explanation." Even as I spoke, I wasn't sure I believed the words myself.

"What in the twelve goddess-be-danged dimensions happened here?" asked a voice that could cut trees into toothpicks.

Lea and I stiffened, pulling apart to face Sebille.

The sprite was striding toward us across the lot, a pair of orange palazzo pants with giant turquoise dots on them swishing around her bony legs. She wore a purple tunic top with oversized pockets and a pair of red sneakers instead of the Wicked Witch of the West shoes she generally wore. She was a colorful, angry rocket, firing our way.

"Meow!" Mr. Wicked proclaimed from down by my feet. He barely touched my ankles as he scurried past me into the battered building, his tail high and whipping the air.

"Sebille," I said, my tone as gentle as I could make it.

She narrowed her eyes, stiffening. "You're using your kindly voice?" she asked, clearly appalled. "On me?" A frown puckered her long, freckled face. "What did you do?"

I shook my head, wishing it was as simple as me messing up. But when Sebille cocked her skinny hip, her belligerence thickening, I realized it didn't matter who she blamed. What mattered was that... My treacherous lip quivered. Tears flooded my blue gaze. "I'm so sorry."

The first cracks appeared in Sebille's protective belligerence. Her glower smoothed out and her eyes widened. She looked at Lea and took note of her red eyes and wet cheeks.

The sprite ran past us, ducking into the destroyed greenhouse. "Mom!"

Lea gave a soft sob. She pushed past me, probably intending to soothe Sebille.

I wanted to believe we could make the sprite feel better. But after working closely with my perpetually angry assistant for nearly five years, I knew that soothing Sebille wasn't going to happen. At least not until she'd torn her way through a few physical objects, laying waste to everything in her path, Viking style. After that, she might stop marauding long enough to have a sad moment.

Sebille outran emotion whenever possible. And when she couldn't outrun it, she usually tried to bludgeon it to death.

I glanced around in panic. While I'd been contemplating the unstoppable force of Sebille's rage, my friend had thrown herself into the lion's den. "Lea!" I hurried through the empty doorway in search of my two friends. One to rescue, and the other to try to wrangle into a targeted weapon, rather than a level ten hurricane flattening everything in its path.

Something exploded at the back of the structure, sending dirt and chunks of tree sky high. The fresh scent of apple filled the air just before a sweet, juicy missile smacked me between the eyes.

Lea yelped. Wicked yowled his displeasure. And Sebille succumbed to a hearty bout of feral rage screaming.

I ran toward the back of the greenhouse, skidding to a stop at the sight of Lea clutching Wally protectively against her chest and Sebille blasting the bat snot out of a large rock. Her freckled face was flushed purple and her bright-red hair, twined into a single, waist-length braid, was covered in rock dust.

Lea turned to me with a look of concern on her face.

I pulled air into my lungs, closed my eyes, and opened them again as I released the breath on a prayer for strength.

"Meow!" Wicked yowled from atop a broken apple tree. Glancing his way, I took note of the agitated slash of his tail and the fur standing at attention over his entire body. I frowned at the sight. Sebille was even scaring him.

The sprite blasted another rock, screaming like a banshee. I stepped forward, not sure what I was going to do. If she were a normal person, I'd give her a hug.

But since she was Sebille...

"Sebille," I said, my voice soft so as not to spook her.

"Arrrrrrrrrr!" she screamed again and threw her hands toward the sky, giving the tattered remains of the ceiling a double-barreled blast. We ran for cover, ducking under the remnants of a pear tree as large and small pieces of metal roofing dropped down on us. Wicked jumped from the tree and ran to me, his pretty orange eyes wide with alarm.

I snatched him up and held him close as the last of the debris slammed to the ground.

Silence throbbed through the building. Lea and I shared another look.

A soft sob filtered through the dusty air and I closed my eyes, my heart breaking for my friend. I dared a glance in her direction, finding her standing with her hands clenched into fists, her head down and her shoulders shaking with silent sobs.

I started toward her.

Wicked leaped from my arms on a yowl and hit the ground with a hiss. He was puffed to twice his normal size. And he was staring toward the empty doorframe.

Not at Sebille.

I reached a hand out to touch Lea's arm, nodding at my cat.

She frowned. "What is..."

A footfall scuffed against the rocky ground outside, tiny stones dancing away to ping against a metal wall. I held up a hand to stop her, a deep sense of foreboding filling me.

My instincts screamed at me to run, though I had no reason to assume the worst.

Except for Wicked's continued yowling and hissing. Behavior which, I had to admit, was an unhappy portent.

Then the doorframe darkened as a tall figure filled it.

And I knew why I had a strong desire to run.

2

AH. THAT IS THE CRUX OF THE PROBLEM, ISN'T IT?

The man was well over six feet tall, with black hair and startling blue eyes. His longish sideburns and beard were touched heavily in gray, the tidy beard on his square chin darkening to black in a wide strip from his full lips to his dimpled chin.

At approximately six feet four and two hundred fifty pounds of pure muscle, the patriarch of the Quilleran clan was an imposing figure. But his intense dark blue gaze and imposing size didn't represent Jacob Quilleran's true power. That power was threaded through the arrogance in his handsome face, and honed to perfection in the power of his beautiful voice.

"We meet again, Keeper." His voice ricocheted off the devastation, rippling over my skin like cool water over smooth rocks. Despite my desire to appear unconcerned by his presence, I gave an involuntary twitch at the sound.

"Jacob," I said in a voice only slightly strangled by fear. "I see you found a way to escape the abyss."

My friends and I had locked Jacob Quilleran away in a

pocket realm fed by the Book of Pages, which served as a portal to places both real and built from imagination. The construct of the realm where we'd stranded the evil witch had been created by my friend Rustin, Jacob's nephew. Rustin had been the victim of his uncle's unfettered ambition in testing a truly evil spell that would have changed the witching world forever.

In short, they'd removed his soul and stuck it into a frog. A truly mouthy frog as it turned out. I'd probably never know if Mr. Slimy's sassy demeanor was the result of Rustin's temporary residence, or an innate feature of his own froggy personality. Either way, it was darned annoying at times.

Fortunately, his aunt and cousin had been able to separate Rustin from his froggy prison, eventually creating for him a dual physical form that served him well. But our attempt to rid the world of his uncle had apparently not worked out quite as planned.

Jacob's smile was smug. "Rumors of my banishment were greatly exaggerated," he agreed. "Someone very helpfully created a crack in the magic keeping me there." His smile told me he knew who that "someone" was.

I winced inwardly. *Troll boogers!* Using the Book of Pages incorrectly to escape a gateway realm, my friends and I had accidentally created a rift in the void that allowed a bunch of monsters to escape.

Apparently, Jacob Quilleran had been one of those monsters.

The witch strode forward, his manner leisurely as he took in the devastation of the greenhouse. I doubted that the timing of his arrival back in our lives was a coincidence.

Beside me, Lea stood with her arms out, fingers dancing

on the air as she created a complex web. I forced myself to stay where I was, so I could protect her if Jacob made a move. It took everything I had to hold my position. I knew how much power Jacob Quilleran had. He carried more magic in his pinkie finger than I possessed in my entire, five-foot-nine-inch fluffy form.

If only fluff transformed into magical ability. I could rule the world.

"Stay back," I told the witch, yanking my own keeper magic forward to dance at my fingertips. It wasn't defensive magic. If I was lucky, it would be enough to make him wet his pants. But I was in close proximity to the artifact library, so my magic had more "umph" than it normally would have.

Ignoring me, the witch took two more long strides in our direction.

I lifted my hands, magic dancing on the air in front of them. "I'm warning you..."

To his credit, Jacob didn't laugh at me. Not really. But his well-formed lips curved slightly at the corners. "What do you think you're going to do with that?" he asked, one dark brow peaked with derision.

"Take another step and you'll find out."

His grin widening, he cast a speculative look at Lea. "That one does have possibilities." Then he shook his head. Flicking the fingers of one hand at Lea, he dispelled the web she'd been creating, exploding it into a hundred tiny pieces that drifted away from her into the branches of the lone, intact pear tree.

Lea growled softly and her fingers started to weave another hex.

I stepped in front of her, hoping to block his vision of what she was doing. What we needed was a distraction.

Lifting my hands, I swung them around to indicate the greenhouse. "I suppose this is your handiwork?"

He glanced around, his blue gaze taking in the mess around him. "I feel as if it would be bragging to take the credit." He nodded as if answering a question present in his own mind. "But yes. It was me." He flashed perfect white teeth, clearly proud of his handiwork.

Behind me, Lea made a soft sound of outrage. I might have growled a little myself. "What have you done with Queen Sindra and the fairies?"

"Ah, that is the crux of the problem, isn't it?" Jacob tapped his dimpled chin with a fingertip. "They were here and now they aren't. This..." he lifted his arms as if to indicate the broken plants and building. "...is so much less important than the lives of all those fairies." He drew out the word "all", lingering on it with obvious pleasure. "We definitely need to get to the bottom of their disappearance. Are they dead? Have they simply gone walk-about? Who knows?"

A soft sound was all the warning I got that Sebille had arrived. I started to turn as she shoved past me, her hands up and magic roiling around them. "Quilleran, you're going to die for this."

Jacob looked startled when Sebille flung a wave of magic energy at him. She'd caught him off guard and the magic slammed into him, throwing him backward into the broken end wall. The wooden frame gave way under the force of the impact and Jacob sprang right up, managing to lift an arm to answer her attack, but Sebille was already there, a growl throbbing in her slender throat as she leaped into the air and slammed into him, sending them both smashing against the wall again. More structural lumber gave way and the building groaned, slowly buckling downward as the metal walls gave out under the weight of the ceiling and the remaining structure.

Light flashed and Sebille made a soft sound of pain as she flew off Jacob and sailed across the building. Her skinny form slapped against the remains of a broken apple tree and slumped, draping over the only remaining branch.

"Sebille!" I started to go to the sprite but Lea grabbed my arm. "I'll do it. My healing magic is better."

I nodded, relieved, until I realized that left me standing alone against the powerful witch. I watched Jacob slide gracefully to his feet, the soft glow of magic assisting the athletic move. Keeper energy danced in my palms and I considered my best course of action. I could call an artifact from the artifact library. Blackbeard's sword had made short work of the witch the last time we'd faced off. But Jacob had been tired then, overwhelmed by the magical strength of several witches and me.

I had a feeling he wouldn't be nearly as easy to defeat in the current situation.

The witch's lips curved and it wasn't a nice smile. "I think we've had enough small talk for now," he said, his blue eyes alight. "How about we get down to business?"

I narrowed my eyes on him. "How about we do that. What is it going to take to get the fairies back?"

He tilted his dark head. "I'm impressed, Keeper. Anyone else would assume they were gone...exterminated...disintegrated into the sands of time."

"No. I don't think so. If you'd killed them all, you'd lose your leverage. Since you're talking instead of attacking, I'm also assuming you need our help with something. So, stop trying to be clever and spit it out. What do you want?"

The light in his eyes flared with delight. He stood with

his legs set apart, his hands folded together in front of him. He threw Sebille a look, a smug smile tugging at his lips.

In that moment, I would have given anything to take Blackbeard's sword to him again. Alas, he'd absconded with the fairies, which meant we had to play nice until we figured out where they were.

And then all bets would be off.

He opened his smug lips and sent me into a spiral of fear and despair. "Yes, Naida keeper. I do need your help. Your... special help. I need you to retrieve an artifact for me."

I raised my brows, feeling the world start to open up beneath my feet. Jacob Quilleran wouldn't have gone to so much trouble for a normal artifact. Whatever he wanted had to be powerful. And dangerous. "What artifact?" I asked, proud to have kept the quaver out of my voice.

"It's a very special artifact, as I'm sure you've figured out."

"What. Is. It?" I bit out, impatience riding my voice.

Jacob inclined his head, seemingly acknowledging my displeasure. "The rune key."

Someone gasped behind me. I turned to find Lea standing with her hand over her mouth, her eyes too wide in her face. Beside her, Sebille appeared slightly the worse for her battle with Jacob, but the rage stiffening her posture didn't look as if it had lessened.

She stepped up next to me, her fists still clenched at her sides. When she spoke, it was as if she were wrenching each word from between steel jaws. "You absconded with the queen of the Enchanted fairies and you think we're going to give you the most important magical artifact in the Universe?"

"I think that's exactly what you're going to do," Jacob said, his self-assured smile widening. He moved closer, lowering his head and looking at Sebille from beneath the dark slash of his brows. "If you ever want to see them again."

"Where are they?" Lea asked, stepping forward. She moved closer to Sebille, no doubt intending to keep our friend from getting herself killed.

I didn't expect the witch to tell us, but he surprised me. "They are currently just a bunch of motes, floating in an energy-charged bubble of my own making. They are nothing but neurons and electrons, all mixed up in a primordial drift of air currents. You cannot rescue them."

Tears burned my eyes and I blinked rapidly to stop them.

Sebille was growling again, but a fine tremor had taken over her skinny form, giving away her fear and sadness. "I'll kill you," she promised.

Jacob held up a hand. "Don't go getting your psychedelic panties in a twist," Jacob said dismissively. "Just get me the key and I'll make them as good as new."

So simple. I glowered at him. "The key doesn't exist in a known dimension." I told him. "We can't get it."

"Ah, but you must."

I looked at Sebille, praying she knew where it was.

She didn't even glance at me. Her expression throbbed with rage, her every feature defined by it. "The Universe holds the key," she told me, her words still taut with emotion. "It's under the highest maximum security. Nobody can get to the key."

The "Universe" was a shared governing body that ruled all the realms from an undetermined central location. The Universal Council kept watch over all of the dimensional representatives, which included Keepers of the Artifacts and the Powers that Be. The Société of Dire Magic was the judicial arm of the governing body. Its members worked with

the police of each realm to make sure the magical population minded their Ps and Qs.

"You'd better hope you're wrong, cranky little sprite. Or
you'll never see your lovely mother again." His smile was an
evil pledge. "I'll be in touch once you have it."

And with a snap of his fingers, Jacob Quilleran
disappeared.

3

DON'T BE A DRAMA QUEEN

Sebille, Lea, and I entered Croakies through the large door in the library. We sucked back in surprise as a body flew past in front of us, skinny arms and legs flailing against the air.

Hobs slammed into one of the massive shelf systems containing magical artifacts, his skinny body folding bonelessly as he slumped to the ground. A beat later, his head came up and his blue eyes widened with delight. "Again!"

I expelled a breath as the little hobgoblin jumped to his feet and ran back past us. All eyes turned to the small cannon across the room, and the pretty little brownie standing beside it with a rammer.

Baca's brown eyes went wide when she found us all staring at her and she dropped the ramming pole, disappearing with a small pop of displaced air.

Sebille stalked past me, bumping my shoulder and striding on by without a glance. Her skinny form was stiff with rage, but her long, freckled face held more than a trace of grief to go with the anger.

"What are you going to do?" I asked the sprite.

She didn't respond. She rounded the ancient standing mirror and yanked off the covering. I'd started covering the mirror after having a truly terrifying doppelganger experience.

Lea and I stopped nearby and watched. The air was thick with tension as Sebille sent a wave of magic into the mirror. A moment later, the silvered surface of the glass rolled into black before slowly morphing into a room that was all too familiar. "Sebille, do you think this is a good idea?" Lea asked.

"She's his sister. If anyone can control him, it's her," Sebille growled back.

I caught movement in the background and snapped my gaze up to the stag's head on the wall above the fireplace. Felonius's gaze followed me whenever I came near, but I hadn't been able to catch him in the act. One day I would catch the stag watching me. When that happened, I fully intended to let him know I'd seen him looking.

From what Rustin's cousin Maude had told me, that would surely put a crimp in the creature's day. As soon as I had the thought, I felt shame. Being a bodiless head on the wall was crimp enough for a lifetime. I suddenly wanted to know Felonius's story, and determined to ask Maude about it when the current crisis was over.

By the time I snapped my attention back to the problem at hand, Madeline Quilleran's living room was fully formed on the surface of the communicating mirror and I could hear soft footfalls heading toward the mirror.

Sebille quietly fumed as Madeline's Natasha Addams-esque form finally came into view. "Princess Sebille." The witch frowned. "Why are you calling me?"

A large raven fluttered into view and landed on Madeline's shoulder, smacking her on the cheek with a fluttering wing.

Madeline glowered at the bird.

"Sorry," Rasputin said in his clipped, Russian accent. "My bad."

"Yes, you are," Maddie agreed.

"Your brother is back," Sebille said, ignoring their banter. "And he's taken all the fairies."

Madeline's surprised expression answered my first question. She hadn't known of Jacob's plans. "Took them? Where? How?"

I stepped up next to Sebille and explained what had happened. "He says they're..." I slid Sebille a look, not wanting to risk setting her off again. One destroyed building in a day was more than enough. "...he says he's got them in an interspace realm. He's using them as leverage."

Maddie's delicate brows lifted. "For what?"

I could feel Lea's gaze burning a spot between my shoulder blades. When I didn't answer right away, Sebille centered her glare on me. "Tell her, Naida. Maybe she can help."

I knew it was my place to ask Madeline for help. I was the KoA, Keeper of the Artifacts for the earthly realm. Maddie was a Power That Be. PTBs answered only to the governing board of the Universe. Her job was to police magical issues that threatened the Universe. She needed to know what Jacob was after. But if I told her, she'd be duty-bound to try and stop us.

Sebille knew this. But she wasn't thinking clearly.

"He wants me to get an artifact for him."

Madeline frowned. "What kind of artifact?"

I chewed the inside of my lip for a beat and then opened my mouth and lied...because I didn't know what else to do.

"He hasn't told us yet. He's playing games. We were wondering if you knew where he was."

Madeline's gaze narrowed on me. She'd probably sensed that I was lying. She seemed to know everything that happened, usually before we did. But she didn't call me on it. Instead, she snickered. "You don't think you can go up against Jacob, do you? That would be a death sentence."

"We have Rustin," Sebille said. "And Lea."

Behind us, Lea waved. "Hey, Maddie."

Madeline's icy demeanor melted slightly when she looked at my friend. Lea had that effect on people. "Hello, Mistress Witch." Maddie thought for a moment and then shook her head. "No. Even with my nephew and the very talented Lea, you will be at a severe disadvantage against Jacob. I'll deal with him."

"If you go after him, he won't tell us where my mother is." Sebille tugged on the long, fire-engine-red braid, her iridescent green eyes looking duller than usual under the weight of fear and grief. "She'll be lost forever." Somewhere along the line, Sebille's fire seemed to have gone out, leaving her shaky. Her voice was clogged with tears.

I resisted the impulse to hug her, knowing it wouldn't go over well. "Sebille's right, Madeline," I said. "If you go after Jacob, he'll know it was because of us and he'll take it out on Queen Sindra and the fairies. We can't take that chance."

Madeline thought about it for a moment, one long finger caressing Rasputin's glossy feathers. The raven was surprisingly quiet, given that his favorite pastime was annoying us. "Why did you contact me?" She addressed her question to Sebille, her tone not unkind.

The sprite stared at her hands, the pale fingers nervously twining. A moment passed as I wondered the same thing. Why *had* she contacted Madeline?

Finally, Sebille looked up, her gaze no longer shimmering with tears. She raised her chin and squared her shoulders. "I need you to find my mother and the fairies. If Jacob could turn them into motes, you should be able to put them back together again. You're more powerful than he is by far."

I barely kept my eyes from widening. Sebille, engaging in flattery? That was a first. She wasn't wrong...exactly. In a battle between Jacob Quilleran and his powerful sister, I wouldn't know what to expect. Jacob was ruthless in his magical use, wringing every drop of magic from his evil core to get what he wanted. Madeline could be ruthless too, but as PTB she knew she had to toe the line or face consequences.

Magic for magic, the two were very closely matched. But Jacob wasn't bound by anything. Not rules or feelings or fear. He was beyond ruthless, and I doubted anyone could stop him without becoming as heartless as he was. Maddie had gotten good at bending, if not breaking the rules, but I wasn't sure she could bend them far enough to meet her brother equally on the field of magical battle.

Madeline's lips pursed in thought. "Tell me the truth about the artifact he wants."

I jolted, guilt washing over my face before I could stop it. "I..."

"Don't lie to me!" Madeline barked out, her visage turning murderous in the blink of an eye. Madeline might not be as ruthless as her brother, but she was plenty hard-nosed enough to deal with me.

"I can't tell you that," I finally said. "I'm sorry."

"He wants the rune key, doesn't he?"

Lea, Sebille, and I shared a look. Finally, I sighed. "I'm not sure..."

Madeline shushed me with a flick of her fingers. "Don't bother prevaricating, Keeper. I know my brother. He wouldn't bother shaking you down for anything less than the rune key. He can get anything else on his own with far less fuss."

She seemed surprisingly calm about the fact that Jacob Quilleran had asked me to steal the greatest artifact of all. As little as I knew about magic in general and the Universe in specific, given my negligent upbringing, even I knew about the rune key. The one artifact that could open any type of magic in existence. Owning it would be indescribably deadly in the hands of someone like Jacob Quilleran. "You seem pretty calm about it," I couldn't help saying.

Madeline shrugged. "There's nothing to get into a dither about, Naida keeper. There's no way in the literal Universe that you will succeed in stealing the key."

I blinked at her. Just like that, she dismissed my nearly certain failure and demise or imprisonment as unimportant. Not to mention the deaths of Queen Sindra and all the fairies under her queendom. Anger surged, heating my face. "You don't care at all about the consequences of this?"

A matching anger pinkened Madeline's cheeks. I had a moment to hate her for how the delicate color just made her look more beautiful. I could feel my face turning purple and swelling until I was sure I looked like an eggplant.

To my shock, Madeline rolled her eyes. I felt mine widening. Had I dropped into opposite world?

"Naida keeper, don't be a drama queen. I intend to get the fairies back safely. And you won't be in any danger because you're not going after the key." Madeline shifted slightly and Rasputin lifted into the air with a caw, his glossy wings flapping as he flew away. "Stay tuned. I'll get back to you when I know something."

Sebille and I opened our mouths to argue, but Madeline had already left the mirror. I stared at the quickly re-silvering surface, only a portion of the witch's living room still visible.

Sebille growled out her frustration and stalked toward the artifact stacks.

As I turned back to the mirror, I saw motion and my gaze snapped to Felonius. I gasped as the stag looked right into my eyes, and winked. Then he was gone as the mirror returned to normal, leaving me looking at my own reflection in the mirror.

"What do you think she's going to do?" Lea asked.

I shook my head, my thoughts spinning. After a beat, I said. "She's going to go after Jacob, despite what we said."

Lea nodded. "I think so too. What should we do?"

Glancing in the direction Sebille had gone, I frowned. There was no way the sprite would just sit tight and wait for someone else to get back to her. If I didn't do something, Sebille was going to go after that key alone and get herself killed. Pulling air into my lungs, I released it slowly. "While Jacob and Madeline keep each other busy, we're going to go after that key."

My phone rang and I glanced at the name on the screen. Despite everything, a small smile found my face. I hit the Answer button. "Hey."

Lea's eyebrows danced at the warm tone of my greeting.

"Hey yourself," my favorite gargoyle responded. "Are you busy tonight?"

I glanced at Lea, chewing the inside of my lip. "Um... actually. I've got to go after an artifact. What's going on?"

He sighed. "I need your help with something. It shouldn't take long. Can you spare me an hour? Maybe two?"

Pacing the library while I considered, I realized I would need Grym's help with the key. The thought made my stomach tighten with dread. I was going to get my friends killed if I wasn't careful. "Sure. I need to talk to you about something anyway."

"Great. I'll pick you up in an hour."

I hung up and found Lea staring at me, looking surprised. "You're going on a date? Now?"

"Of course not. Grym needs my help with an artifact. I'm going to ask for his advice on getting the key. Don't worry," I told her with a smile. "I'll stay on task."

Lea nodded. "I'll do some research too." Her expression tightened. "Do you think we can ask Rustin for help? Will he go against Madeline's wishes to help us?"

Something slammed into the back door of the library and we jumped. High-pitched giggling ensued and we both relaxed. Hobs and Baca scampered across the room and disappeared into the stacks, leaving a trail of their happy, excited voices behind them.

Lea wrung her hands, her round face filled with worry. "I'm a giant ball of stress. If we have to break into the vault at the Universe to get the key..." She shook her head.

"We're going to figure it out," I promised. "We have a lot of friends who can help."

"But we can't ask them to do it, Naida," Lea said. Her turquoise gaze glistening with unshed tears. "We probably won't survive. We can't ask them to take that risk."

"Hey." I walked over and pulled her into a hug. "You don't have to go. Sebille and I can handle this."

She barked out a watery laugh. "That would be something to see. Sebille steamrolling her way through every obstacle and you blasting everybody with bladder draining magic."

My smile felt tight on my face. "Hey, that's a good weapon. You 're discounting the trauma-inducing effects of peeing your pants in front of other people."

My magic might not be defensive. The most it could do was curl my victim's hair or make them pee themselves. But I had control of thousands of artifacts. Any number of them were plenty defensive for what we'd need. The trick would be in choosing wisely for the trip.

"It will be fine," I told her. "You can stay here with Wicked and Hex...keep an eye on Hobs and Baca."

She shook her head emphatically, her glossy curls dancing around her shoulders. "I'm not deserting you and Sebille. I'm going. I just think we'll want to be very careful about who we bring. What doesn't kill us on this journey might get us thrown into Casa De Grimoire."

Casa De Grimoire was the cute little name the magical population used for the Société of Dire Magic's prison system. Thinking of the Société increased my stress level. The organization was tasked with finding and punishing those who misused magic or used it for dire purposes. I was pretty sure what we were about to do would fall under both of those categories.

"We're not going to fly into this without giving serious consideration to what we're doing," I assured my friend. "There has to be a way to give Jacob what he thinks he wants, without giving him the actual key."

Lea didn't look convinced, but she nodded. "I'm going home to start researching. I'll call you in the morning if I find anything."

I gave her a last hug and watched her leave, my heart heavy. Throwing another glance in the direction Sebille had gone, I headed upstairs to my apartment so I could get ready to meet my boyfriend, Detective Wise Grym.

4

IT WAS A DARK AND STORMY NIGHT...

I stood looking down at the artifact, frowning. "What is that?" I asked, cocking my head in case it would look more familiar from that angle. It didn't.

"I was told it was a typewriter. An ancient artifact." Grym reached a tentative finger out and poked the metallic black device. Nothing happened for a moment. Then, there was a soft whirring sound, and two of the keys depressed.

We both stared at the sheet of paper stuck into the top. "*It...*" I read. "Okay."

The keys took off in a spasm of rapid movement. Grym and I leaned over the thing, watching the tidy black letters hit the paper.

"It was a dark and stormy night," Grym read. "That's strange..."

The room turned pitch black. A boom rattled the windows and I jumped with an unmanly yelp. "What in the world?"

A jagged slash of light flared beyond the windows and a monsoon-like downpour pounded against the roof.

"Do you have a...bag?" Grym yelled.

He was inches from my face, but I barely heard him through the cacophony of the storm.

Still, I knew what he was asking. I nodded, sticking a hand into my oversized purse and pulling out a magic dampening bag.

Grym and I stared at it for a beat, then shared a grimace. I only knew he'd grimaced because a too-close flash of lightning briefly illuminated the room.

The sound of keys clacking rose above the storm, clear as day. I pulled out my cell and turned on its flashlight, illuminating the sheet of paper.

But that didn't stop the two men from breaking into the house to kill its inhabitants.

Grym and I shared a wide-eyed look. Grym reached for his gun just as the front door burst open, slivers of wood flying away from its shattered frame.

Two massive figures stood in the doorway, their eyes gleaming with hostility in the intermittent illumination of the deadly lightning strikes.

I backed away, energy spitting at my fingertips. "Um, Grym?"

He lifted his gun, shoving me behind him. "Hands up. Drop your...weapons," he demanded.

I peered around my boyfriend and saw the first man stride through the door, a crutch gripped in his hands.

Keys started to clack again.

Using inhuman speed and unnatural grace, the men disarmed the man of his gun.

Grym grunted in pain. The man with the crutch had crossed the room in the time it took for me to blink. He smacked Grym's gun hand so fast I couldn't follow his movements, then he spun on the tips of his toes, like a Prima

Ballerina, and whacked the back of Grym's knees, sending him crashing to the floor.

Keys clacked.

Energy spit from the woman's hands and the intruder wet himself.

Great idea, I thought. "Happy to oblige," I said as I threw my keeper magic at the man with the crutch. He bent double, his hands covering his "no, no square". He turned and ran from the room as a dark stain spread beneath his hands.

The second man charged, an ugly brass lamp in his hands, and tried to smack me in the head with it. He got a snoot full of my magic and stopped, slowly looking down at the giant wet spot in his khakis. He looked at me and dropped the lamp. "You're the devil."

I shrugged. "I've been called worse."

He turned and ran like his friend.

Grym got to his feet with a groan. "Nice work, Penelope PeePee."

I snorted, blowing on the tips of my fingers.

Boom! Thunder rattled the tiny house.

Whoosh! Lightning flashed.

Clack, clack, clack. Keys depressed at a phenomenal speed.

Grym and I glanced toward the paper and groaned.

Four more intruders joined the party.

Large shapes filled the doorway again.

Grym looked at me. "I've got this. You need to disable that thing so it can't type anything else."

I nodded. "Penelope PeePee is on the case."

Grym ran toward the four newcomers.

I bathed the strange storytelling machine with light from my phone, looking for a button to cut the power.

Across the room the sound of fists hitting flesh, grunts of pain, and the occasional heartfelt swear played out with the cacophony of the still-raging storm as a soundtrack.

I squinted down at the devious device. "Where is your power button?" I asked it.

I jumped as keys clacked inches from my nose.

Four more intruders arrived.

"No!" I yelled.

"Naida!" Grym bellowed.

"Sorry!"

A flash of light told me Grym had assumed his gargoyle form. In that form, he had a fighting chance of beating off eight full-sized men. I only hoped the intruders were either made-up people or had magic of their own, or we'd just created a whole "non-magic human discovers that the boogie man lives" thing we'd have to deal with later.

Clack, clack, clack.

One of the intruders was a rock climber and he buried a piton in the gargoyle's side.

Grym screamed, the sound making my skin crawl.

"That's it!" I yelled at the monstrous machine. "You're going down."

Clack, clack, clackity clack.

The woman doubled over with pain from an episode of irritable bowel.

Agony seared through my belly and I yelped, bending double as I waited it out. "You jerk," I growled out in between breath-stealing waves of pain.

Clack, clack.

Sticks and stones...

"Good idea," I growled, picking up the first intruder's discarded crutch. Agony gripped my gut and I gritted my teeth, raising the crutch above the machine. "Clack this!" I told it. "Woman beats the devil machine senseless," I said.

An arm at the side of the machine swung sideways with a swishing sound. It glanced off my knuckles, taking some skin with it. "Ow!" I raised the crutch again.

Agony flared through my belly.

Clack, clack, clack.

Mystery malady?

Heat flashed through me, sliding from my belly all the way up to the top of my head. Sweat coated my skin and dampened the roots of my hair. I felt like I was going to combust.

Hot flashes. "Dirty pool!" I yelled, dropping the crutch and yanking the machine's arm-thingy several times in a hot-flash-induced rage.

"Naida!"

I glanced at Grym and found him covered in intruders. Panic joined the irritable bowel and hot flashes to turn me into a crazy lady. "I'm done playing nice," I told the thing as I wrapped my hands around it and lifted it off the table.

Clack, clack, clack, clack, clack...

Six more intruders ran into the house.

The clacking sped up, sounding slightly frantic. I didn't care. My heart was hardened behind a wall of discomfort and pain. "You're goin' down." I shoved it toward a too-small magic dampening bag, splitting the seams and not caring.

Clackity clack.

The living room caught on fire.

Sure enough, flames shot skyward from the carpet, caught on the drapes and took off like a kid at a playground.

I pulled a second bag over the other end, tugging and twisting until most of the thing was covered. The arm tried to move but the bag stopped it. I dug in my purse for tape, knowing I wouldn't find any, but came out with a metal container of bandages in assorted sizes.

Sweat ran off me as I panted, thinking about how good the rain outside would feel on my over-heated skin. I pulled the edges of the two bags together and slapped an oversized bandage over it.

Whump, whump, whump. The arm bowed the bag, trying to escape.

Pain sliced through my middle. I stopped, bent double, and groaned until it passed. "Irritable bowel. That's some tenth-level evil stuff right there," I mumbled to myself.

Clack...

The muffled sound of the keys trying to type made me smile. "You're done, sucker."

I tugged another section of edges together and slapped on a large bandage to seal it.

There was only one small section left open.

Clack, clack, clack.

The woman got a giant pimple.

I felt it burst onto my nose. It felt like Mount Enchanted. Reaching up, I touched the biggest pimple I'd ever felt. Tears burned my eyes. "I hate you," I told the machine.

Cl, cl, cl...

I tugged the last section closed and slapped my last bandage over it.

The sounds of fighting stopped.

The flames in the room died out. The thunder stopped. The lightning sizzled away. The constant drone of rain eased into nothing.

And my stomach stopped hurting.

I sagged to the ground, panting. Shoving a sweaty hunk of my hair off my oily face, I closed my eyes and tried to remember why I'd thought being an artifact keeper was a good idea.

As I became aware of the silence, my eyes popped open. I searched the darkness for Grym, panic starting to rise.

The lights came on and I yelped. He was standing only a couple of feet away from me. Three pitons stuck out of his body and his dark eyes were filled with pain as well as anger. Nevertheless, I watched as his expression changed to horror when it landed on me. "Ugh! What's that on your face?" he asked. "And why are you all sweaty?"

5
***

EH TU, BRUTE?

Grym dropped me off at Croakies with an apologetic kiss. "Feel better," he told me, earning himself a frown. He'd dug himself a hole to China by not only noticing but commenting on the currently mountainous geography of my nose and the "dewy" quality of my skin from the hot flashes.

If he really loved me, he'd have pretended not to notice. Yes, I do believe that ignorance is bliss. I'd have preferred to pretend I wasn't currently as repulsive as a slug in his eyes. Unfortunately, he'd taken that option away from me. The knowledge left me feeling cranky.

I stalked toward the front door and opened it before I realized I'd forgotten to talk to him about our trip to the Universe's vault. I spun around in time to watch him wave and pull away.

Sighing, I shoved the door open and went inside. Locking and warding the bookstore door, I sagged with weariness. I was going to drop the spelled typewriter in the toxic artifact vault and have a quick shower before falling into bed. I'd need my rest to tackle what was coming.

MORNING DAWNED MUCH TOO QUICKLY, leaving me feeling sloggy and still a little cranky from the night's escapades. Fortunately for me, I could never out-cranky the sprite. As soon as she joined me in the bookstore, my mood took a back burner to hers.

"Did you sleep okay?" I asked.

Sebille's upper lip curled in a snarl.

Alrighty then.

"I'll just..." I pointed toward the back of the book stacks. "I have some books to shelve."

A low growl followed me to the books.

We passed the early morning hours in silence, as far away from each other as possible. Finally, I heard the front door open and slam closed and looked out the picture window at the front of the store to see Sebille stalking down the sidewalk.

I hurried outside, worried she was going after Jacob. "Hey!" I yelled.

My assistant jolted to a stop and turned a murderous look my way. She didn't even bother to speak, she simply peaked a red eyebrow and glowered.

"If you're going to the bakery, I'll take a chocolate glazed...or two."

Her gaze narrowed. "You sure you want to feed that mountain on your nose?"

I paled, my hand flying to cover said mountain. I'd nearly managed to forget it was there. Figured the sprite would mention it just to remind me. I gave her a hopeful look. "Maybe you have some pimple healing magic?"

Sebille rolled her eyes and swung around, stomping on down the sidewalk. I noticed with mixed emotions that her shoulders were less slumped than before. It would be good if she was working herself out of her funk. I just wished she wouldn't do it at my expense.

The door to the shop next door opened and Lea stepped out, a large, leather-bound book in her hands. She looked pretty as usual in a soft pink sweater and a white ankle-length skirt with tiny pink flowers embroidered on it. A small little gray cat that looked a lot like Mr. Wicked followed on her heels. Wicked's litter-mate, Hex, meowed a welcome when she spotted me and trotted over, tail high.

"Good morning, beautiful," I said to the little gray cat, bending to scratch her silky back.

"Right back atchya, gorgeous," Lea said, grinning. She got a good look at me and twitched. "Oh!"

I frowned. "Eh tu, Brute?"

"That's...um...memorable."

"I don't suppose you have anything for it?"

Her smile returned. "I'll bring something over later."

Lea followed me back into the store and Hex took off running toward the dividing door, which I'd left open. I knew the little cat was going in search of Mr. Wicked. "He's still sleeping," I told Hex, "But I think Vel is awake." Vel was the newest member of our little menagerie. We'd rescued her from an evil owner in the demonic realm, who'd also been a Keeper of the Artifacts for the realm...unfortunately.

"Tea?" I asked around a yawn, trudging toward the teapot Sebille had put on to boil. I grimaced, realizing I'd have to make my own tea. Sebille generally made the tea since she was tea-talented. My tea, on the other hand, somehow always tasted like moldy garden dirt.

"Maybe I'll just wait until Sebille gets back," I mumbled to myself.

"No thanks. I found something last night," Lea said. She

settled into a chair at the table and ran a hand over the cover of the book she'd brought.

I sat down across from her. My stomach roared its disapproval of the empty table.

Lea grinned. "Do you want to grab something to eat first?"

"Sebille went to get donuts." I hoped. "What did you find?"

"There's a chapter about the Universe's vault in this textbook." She poked a perfectly manicured fingernail covered in dark brown polish at the book.

I glanced at the title etched into the maroon leather tome. "Unique and Important Magical Structures?"

She nodded. "It's surprisingly informative." She slid a finger into a spot marked off with a bookmark and opened it. A picture in muted colors dominated the page, the spot unlike anything I'd ever seen before. The foreground was covered in flowers of every color in the rainbow. Dancing among the flowers were oversized butterflies, known as flutterflies I thought, and small winged creatures that might have been pixies. In the distance was a castle, its classic lines rising high into an overcast sky.

"Wow," I breathed.

"I know, right?" Lea agreed. "This is Nom. It's a storage realm."

"Is that where the vault is?"

"That's what the author believes. But nobody's ever seen the vault. It's an urban legend among magic users."

Grimacing, I said, "That doesn't make me very happy."

Lea nodded. "Keep in mind, most urban legends are based on truth of some kind. Nom exists. The vault most likely exists too. But nobody knows what it looks like or where on Nom it's located."

"Who lives in the castle?"

"According to this, nobody does. Most of Nom is rumored to be made up of glamours and constructs. Its sole purpose is said to be protecting The Universe's most valuable and dangerous items."

The front door slammed open, crashing against the wall hard enough to dent the drywall. I glared over at Sebille. "Can you please refrain from bringing the building down around our ears?"

Sebille was staring at a mark on the wall from the door, her posture stiff. She held a large white bakery box and her fingers dented the soft cardboard where they touched it. Her knuckles were white.

Anger faded and compassion replaced it. I stood up and walked over to Sebille, taking the box from her hands. "We're going to get them back," I told her.

To my shock, tears glistened in her dazzling green gaze. "I can't feel her." She poked her flat chest. "Here."

All the air left my lungs. My vision blurred under my own tears. I pulled her into a one-armed hug and, to my surprise, she allowed it. "I'm so sorry, Sebille. But I'm going to do everything I can to get her back. You have my word on that."

She sniffled and nodded, pulling away. "I'll make tea."

OUR FIRST ORDER of business was figuring out who we needed to take with us. This was complicated by the need to keep our team as small as possible. Which meant we needed to maximize our skillsets. Hard to do when we had no idea what we were going to need once we got to Nom. And even harder since we had no idea how we were getting to Nom.

Okay. *New* first order of business...getting to Nom.

"We can't just take a bus or a plane," Sebille said.

"I suppose we could go through the painting again," I said with a grunt of displeasure. The painting in question was a portal to the Universe or, really, any spot in the universe you wanted to go. Though, I had no idea how to select my destination, which made it something of a wild card.

I had a feeling Madeline Quilleran had made sure I'd ended up where I needed to go the one time we'd used it—an alternate dimension outside of my very own store, Croakies. Well, not my store. But one just like mine. That particular Croakies was run by the man who'd named the store *Croakies* initially.

I didn't hold that against him. Much.

Anyway, I'd landed at the correct destination, but I hadn't selected it before I leaped, literally, out of the painting and plummeted to what I was certain would be my death. Mine and Mr. Wicked's. So, it was possible the portal had pulled the intention from my mind.

I just didn't know.

"That all seems too random," Lea said with a grimace. "We're not going to get more than one chance to get this right."

Sebille nodded. "I have an idea for how to get to Nom. Let's move on to the team selection."

I nodded, happy to have our travel plans off my plate. "Okay. So, I'd like to keep the number as small as possible without putting ourselves at a disadvantage magically."

Lea agreed. Sebille frowned.

"What's with the sad face?" I asked the sprite.

She copped an attitude at my question. "I'm not making a face."

I shook my head. "Okay. So, I'm thinking..." I started.

"It's just that, I don't know why we're not going with the best crew we can. After all, like Lea said, we're only getting one shot at this and mother...that is...all the fairies are depending on us."

I bit back a quick response, knowing it would be a mistake to respond without giving it some thought. Finally, I said. "I know this is important. It's the most important thing we've ever done," I told Sebille, trying not to sound like I was just placating her. "But it's also the most dangerous thing we've ever done."

"I don't know," Lea said. "Going back to the Jurassic era was pretty dangerous."

I bobbed my head. "Point taken. But you know what I mean. We've got a lot riding on this, it's true. And everyone we take is going to be in significant physical and potentially legal danger. I'm just trying to limit the damage."

Sebille's belligerent expression didn't soften. "I think we should let them decide," she said. "Personally, I'd be mad if somebody made a decision for me without asking."

I looked at Lea and she gave me a pained smile. "She's not wrong."

I sighed. "Okay. We'll call them all here and tell them what's going on. They can decide if they want to come or not."

Sebille nodded, her expression softening. "Good. Now, here's who I think we should invite."

6

_____

HAVE YOU LOST YOUR MIND?

The bookstore was full of people. All of them were looking expectantly at me, waiting for an explanation for why I'd called them together. Looking out at the questioning faces, I felt nervousness take hold...something that didn't normally happen when facing my friends.

Finally, Rustin spoke. "What happened to your face?"

I narrowed my eyes at him, wishing I could hex him into a toad...again...for picking on my pimple. Lea's herbal mask had taken some of the redness from the mountainous region, and had shrunk it a little. But it was still big enough to have its own zip code. "Never mind the bump..."

"Zit," Sebille said loudly.

You could ski down that thing, said Slimy, the frog.

Grins split on many of the expectant faces.

"Har," I told them all. "I had an unfortunate encounter with a toxic artifact."

Grym nodded in support. "Believe me, that typewriter was no joke."

Rustin burst into laughter. "You were beat up by a typewriter?"

My slitty gaze burned into him. He didn't even notice.

"Bark!" said Vel happily. The little green dog bounced around my feet, her tail whipping the air behind her.

I scratched behind her ears, smiling down at the little demon dog. "At least you love me," I told her in a voice that was perilously close to baby talk. Mr. Wicked would rip a few tracks in my skin if I talked baby talk to him. But Vel didn't seem to mind. In fact, her bright black eyes shone with happiness at the sound of my voice.

"What exactly have you called us here for, Naida?" asked my uncle Archie, a.k.a. Archibald Pudsnecker, Void Keeper for The Universe by way of the Société of Dire Magic. His position was both a plus and a minus, and I wasn't sure if he would help us with our current problem.

I stared at him, knowing his inclusion was the diciest of all. "We have a situation. A bad one. And Sebille, Lea, and I are going on a mission to fix it. We called you all here to ask for opinions, aid, resources."

"What's happened?" asked Theopolis Gargantu, our resident giant. Theo owned the local pawn shop, which was really just a front for his junk collecting habit. His girlfriend, Birte, shared Theo's love of collecting, given that she was a dragon shifter.

I glanced toward Sebille. She held herself stiffly, a more-or-less permanent scowl on her face. She didn't speak up, so I guessed it was up to me. Biting back a sigh, I glanced toward Maude Quilleran. I was hoping the young witch would be a good information source. "Jacob Quilleran is back."

A collective groan filled the room. Maude had been leaning against the shelves, but she straightened, her blue eyes wide with alarm. "Uncle Jacob is here?" She looked around, her slender arms wrapping protectively around her body.

I shook my head. "He's not here...now. But he was earlier. He..."

Apparently taking pity on me, Lea chimed in. "He destroyed the greenhouse and took the fairies."

There was a chorus of gasps, followed by a clash of conversation.

Poor Maude was chalk white. "I have to tell Aunt Maddie."

"She knows," Sebille bit out. "She told us to relax while she fixed it."

Maude chewed her lip, avoiding our gazes. It was clear she was uncomfortable with that idea, though whether it was because she thought Madeline would fail, or because she knew how unreasonable the request was, I didn't know.

"I'm not sitting around waiting for Jacob to defeat Madeline," Sebille said on a growl. "He'll take it out on my mother and the others."

Heads nodded.

I spoke up again. "According to Jacob, Queen Sindra and the fairies have been sent into some kind of pocket world. He claims he'll return them to this realm, unharmed, if we get an artifact for him."

"What artifact?" Grym asked.

I looked into his dark-caramel gaze, seeing the tightness around them that told me he'd already figured out what I was struggling to tell them. "I..."

"Give it up, Naida." Archie said, his British accent thickening with his irritation.

"We..." I sighed, looking away. Revealing our goal for the journey was going to be like flinging an explosive into a fireworks factory. Nobody in that room would understand why we had to do it. Nobody was going to support the effort. No matter the cost.

"What is it, Naida?" Maude asked, her voice soft.

"We're going after the rune key," Sebille declared, her pointy chin held high.

As expected, the room exploded with outrage.

"Are you serious?"

"No! Absolutely not."

"Have you lost your mind?"

"How?"

The last was spoken quietly, the tone firm but unexcited. I looked at my Uncle Archie. His expression was the one he wore when he was looking for the answer to a scientific problem. "What?" I asked.

Archie uncrossed his legs and leaned forward, his sorcerer's robes swinging around his skinny legs. "How do you plan to get your hands on the rune key?"

"Um..."

"We're traveling to Nom," Sebille said, saving me from my suddenly blank mind. "We'll need to break into the vault to get it."

"You can't give Uncle Jacob the rune key!" Rustin said. His piercing blue gaze stabbed angrily in my direction. "Do you have any idea how much damage he could cause with it?"

I opened my mouth to speak but never got a chance.

"Do you think Queen Sindra would want you to put the entire universe in danger to save her?" Grym spoke quietly, his disapproving expression pointed right at me. The sight of it made my chest hurt.

I shook my head. "We..."

"We can't just let him kill them," Maude said. "There has to be a way to save them without giving Jacob the artifact.

Maybe we could give him a fake to get him to release the fairies."

"As I was trying to say, we..."

"A fake isn't something that's easily done," Lea said, her face tight. "I did some research on the key. It isn't meant to ever leave the vault. But, if it *is* removed for some reason, a magical mark within the key ignites. If that mark isn't there, he'll know it's not the real thing."

"What about a four-dimensional glamour?" Theo asked. "We could include the mark."

"Won't work," Lea said. "Nobody knows what the mark looks like, so we can't copy it."

Silence filled the room and I saw my chance. "Here's what we..."

"So, you're just going to hand it over to him?" Birte asked, a soft growl in her voice.

The room erupted into arguing again, the voices growing louder as passions built.

I stuck my fingers between my lips and whistled, the shrill sound slicing into the chaos like a blade. Everybody stopped talking and looked at me. I held up a hand, palm out. "Please let me talk and I'll explain what we're thinking."

They waited in silence.

Taking a deep breath, I laid out the bare bones of our plan. "There are artifacts that can copy anything down to the most minute detail. Our plan is to copy the key inside the vault and bring the copy out of the vault so it receives the mark it needs." I didn't tell them that the chances our copy would fool the vault were slim. I barely even wanted to admit that to myself.

I looked around at our audience, seeing thoughtful looks on a couple of their faces. They were considering the copy option. Grym, however, stood with his arms crossed over his chest, staring daggers at me.

I swallowed hard and went on. "The copy has to have enough magic to fool Jacob, but not enough for him to do any real damage with it."

"How are you going to accomplish that?" Rustin asked.

I nodded. "We have a plan for that. It will involve everybody in this room and a few more, but it's doable." When there were no further interruptions, I went on. "We know we have to escape through the vault door when we leave, but we're hoping we can arrive using a much simpler path."

"The Book of Pages," Maude guessed.

I nodded. We'll need an accurate representation of the interior of the vault." I looked at Archie. "I'm assuming you could get that for us."

He frowned.

"We don't know the protocols for moving through the vault," I said. "That's a problem we need to solve, along with how to deal with the three obstacles we'll face once inside."

"What are *we* doing here?" Theo asked.

I looked at the giant, my stomach tightening at the coldness in his manner. "I know this is dangerous. I understand not everyone will be able to help us. But we've made up our minds. We're doing this." I lifted a hand toward Sebille and Lea. "We'd appreciate any help, guidance, or information you can give us."

"You're not giving Jacob the key?" Uncle Archie asked.

"No." I didn't qualify that with my doubts and the potential for failure, but I had to clamp my teeth together to stop from spilling it all. Archie watched me for a beat and then nodded. "I'm in."

I closed my eyes with relief. When I opened them again, the room shimmered behind unshed tears. "Thank you."

He inclined his head. "We should include your mother and brother."

My heart forgot to beat for a moment. Then, swallowing hard, I said, "Do you think they'll come?"

"If you're going in, we'll all go. Your family will stand with you."

The tears slipped down my face, unheeded. I swallowed past a lump in my throat and nodded.

"I'm not happy about it," Grym said, his expression stony. "But, if you're going, I'm going."

I inclined my head, unable to look him in the eyes.

"I want to go," Maude said.

I barely kept from wincing. "Maude, I don't think..."

"I'm going."

"Madeline will eat my heart if you join us."

The teen grinned. "She wouldn't eat it, but she might tenderize it a bit."

I snorted a laugh, despite the fear engendered at the idea of the young girl joining our deadly journey. "We'll talk about it," I said, fully intending to talk her out of joining.

Theo stood. When I glanced at him, he shook his head. "I'm sorry, Naida. I can't go with you."

Disappointment soured my stomach. I nodded. "I understand."

"If you need help preparing, I'll help. But I can't go to Nom."

The way he said it made me wonder if he was hiding something.

"That would be great, thanks, Theo."

He looked at Birte, who was still seated. She stood slowly, glancing at him before turning to me. "If you need a dragon, I'll come. If not, I'll be happy to add some of my magic to the fake key. Let me know."

I was shocked the dragon would be willing to come with us, particularly since Theo was declining.

"That's wonderful, Birte," I smiled at her. "Can I get back to you once we have a firm plan?"

She nodded.

I watched them leave, my stomach tightening with nerves. What were we doing? We weren't going to survive what we were planning.

"We'll go, Miss," said a small voice from the shelves. I turned to find Hobs and Baca sitting atop the frontmost shelving unit, their tiny hands entwined. "We want to help."

I sniffed, unable to speak through the knot in my throat.

"Rustin?" Sebille asked, her tone sharp.

I swung my gaze toward our friend. His silence suddenly felt ominous.

He was frowning, looking even more unhappy than Grym. After a beat, he lifted his gaze to the sprite. "Have you told Aunt Madeline about this?"

Lea, Sebille, and I shared a look.

Sebille lifted her chin. "Yes."

"And?" Rustin asked.

"And, she told us she'd deal with it."

"Then, why are you moving forward with this ridiculous plan?"

"Because, when she confronts Jacob, he's going to think we asked her to do it," I responded. "And Jacob is going to kill the queen and all the fairies." I let that sit there for a beat, watching as Rustin's frown deepened. "I know this puts you in a difficult situation..." I started to say.

Rustin interrupted. "Yes. It puts us in an untenable position, Naida. And, I'm sorry, but Maude and I can't be involved in this. Not in any way."

"Hey!" Maude objected. "I'm going, Rustin. You don't control me."

Anger flared to life in his eyes. "Maybe I don't, but Madeline does. If you try to join this ridiculous farce, I'll tell her what you're doing." His gaze swung to me. "All of you."

Sebille stepped forward, poking him in the chest as he stood. "I'll be sure and let my mother know how little you cared about the lives of fairies."

He flinched but shook his head. "I'm sorry..."

"Don't bother, Rustin," she said. "You're dead to me."

His jaw tight, Rustin inclined his head and turned away, pulling Maude out of the store with him.

A tense silence filled the room after they left. Then Lea cleared her throat. "We should get started. We have a lot we need to discuss."

7

OY, MORTY!

I stood in the center of the library and closed my eyes, pulling air into my lungs and slowly releasing it. In the distance, through the dividing door, I could hear my friends talking, voices raising and lowering as they hashed out a series of key issues related to our coming adventure.

I was glad to be out of that room. I'd mumbled a promise to search for the right artifacts to bring along, and left them to their squabbling with a sense of deep relief.

We were all tense and unhappy. Nobody wanted to do what needed to be done. But the outcome if we didn't search for the rune key was unacceptable.

I'd do anything I could to get Sebille's people back. Even the impossible and dangerous.

Sighing, I forced my mind back to the present task. I engaged my keeper's magic and ran through the contents of the library. I had ten thousand five hundred and sixty-two artifacts in the library. Each one glowed in my mind with a magical signature I recognized since fully accepting my role as KoA, tying me inextricably to the magic and the library.

Each item had a place and everything was where it was supposed to be.

I pushed past the inventory scrolling through my mind to a different kind of search. I needed to find a specific artifact that would duplicate the rune key well enough to fool Jacob Quilleran.

"Meow." A soft, warm heaviness wrapped around my calves, Mr. Wicked's rumbling purr vibrating soothingly against my skin.

I opened my eyes and looked down at him. "Hey, handsome. I could sure use your help finding this artifact."

Wicked took another pass around my calves, tail whipping the air. "Meow," he said again, as if agreeing to help.

I pushed my doubts away and settled back to my search. Duplication could take many forms.

I had painting artifacts, drawing artifacts, and even a camera that created duplicates of the objects it captured in photos. But I needed more than a surface duplication. I needed something that copied every aspect of the external, internal, and mystical.

I needed a magical 3D printer. But I didn't have one, and I was realizing that I'd been too confident in thinking I would be able to get my hands on the correct artifact.

"Naida?"

My eyes snapped open and I turned my head to watch Grym stride toward me. His dark gaze locked on me and his handsome features were tight with unhappiness.

I tensed, watching his six-foot-tall, wide-shouldered form bear down on me. I didn't want to fight with him because I knew he was right. What we were about to do was dangerous and stupid. But I just didn't think we had a choice.

I shook my head as he neared. "Please don't try to talk me out of this. We need to do it."

"You're going to get yourselves thrown into the Universal Prison. Or worse, die trying to save the fairies."

I narrowed my gaze on him. "Are you implying they're not worth saving?"

He crossed muscular arms across his chest. "You know that's not what I'm saying."

I shook my head. "I really don't know anything," I told him. "Except that I need to do this. You can bow out, Grym. I'll understand if you want to step away from this one."

He expelled air, closing his eyes for a beat. When they snapped open again, the anger was gone and fear had taken its place. "I'm worried about you," he said softly.

"To be honest, I'm worried about all of us. But..."

He held up a large hand. "But you have to do this. I get it. I just don't like it."

My smile met his and I nodded. "It's okay. You don't have to like it. I don't like it either."

He turned his attention to the shelves. The massive stacks rose thirty feet into the air and filled most of the huge warehouse space. "What magic are you going to pull out of here?"

I bit back an impulsive response, which would be that I didn't know. "I'm working on that right now. What do you think of our plan?"

"It's not really a plan, is it?" he asked. "It's the bare bones of an idea. We have a lot of fleshing out to do."

I nodded. He wasn't wrong. "Once I figure out our duplication artifact, I'm hoping we can add the meat to those bones."

"What can I do to help?"

I thought about his question and realized he could be

very helpful. "Can you see if you can find Jacob Quilleran's lair? I'd feel better if we knew where he was. Madeline too. I'm worried she's going to go after her brother and start a war the fairies will pay for with their lives."

He nodded, glancing at his watch. "I should get back to work anyway. I'm the only one working the late shift tonight."

My brows lifted. "You're working alone? Why? Is everybody else sick?"

"No. Things have just been really quiet lately so everybody's taking the vacation time they've been stockpiling."

It *had* been quiet in Enchanted for the last few months. Ever since the night of the blood moon, when things had gotten dangerously squiggy and we'd found ourselves dealing with a moon-sick demon dog and battling a nasty critter from the demonic realm.

Grym leaned in and touched his lips to mine, moving closer and pulling me against his powerful body as he deepened the kiss. I sighed against his lips and let myself lean into him for a long moment. I'd been worried our trip to Nom would break us. Grym was a stickler for the rules, which made him a great cop, but a bit of a challenge when Sebille and I decided to cowboy up and launch into one of our ill-advised missions. Fortunately for us, as a gargoyle, he had a natural protective instinct that ensured he'd be there trying to keep us safe.

I only hoped I didn't get him killed or imprisoned by including him in our rescue mission.

"I'll see you later," he said, tracing my jawline with his warm, lightly calloused finger. "Let me know if you run into trouble." He started to leave but stopped, turning back. "Keep me informed on the timeline for this Nom trip. I'll have to take vacation time."

I nodded, watching him stride away. The man looked just as good going as he had arriving.

A crash sounded at the back of the building, behind the stacks of artifacts. I headed in that direction. "Hobs? Is that you? What are you doing?"

No response. Which wasn't at all like my favorite hobgoblin. "Who's there?" Maybe the brownie was creating havoc all by herself for once. "Baca?"

The sound of two metallic objects clanging together brought me to an abrupt stop. Keeper magic sizzled at my fingertips. I moved forward more slowly, my head on a swivel. "Whoever you are, I'm coming in hot."

I nearly grinned at my own stupidity. Coming in hot. Who says that?

The air in front of me shifted, and the tiny form of a winged creature with vibrant green eyes and waist-length dark red hair appeared. Her image wavered, growing faint for a beat and then gaining density.

I felt my eyes go wide at the sight. "Queen Sindra?"

The tiny figure reached toward me with one minuscule hand, her mouth moving but no sound coming out. She looked as if she existed on a different plane. Likely she did. I let the magic fall away from my fingertips and took a step closer. "We're working on releasing you and your people," I told her, reading fear in her gaze.

To my surprise, the fairy queen shook her head. Her mouth formed a rapid spate of words, but I couldn't hear her and she was speaking too quickly for me to read the words on her lips. "I can't hear you," I said, my heart pounding with frustration and fear. "Can you speak more slowly?"

She buzzed forward, the movement shifting the air and filling my nostrils with the scent of ozone. Hanging a mere two feet in front of my face, Queen Sindra spoke carefully, rounding her lips before she slowly spoke again. I read the words, "help him" there.

"Help him?" I asked. "Who? Jacob?" The name came out in an alarmed squeak. Was Sindra actually telling me to help the witch who'd trapped her in an unknown space between dimensions? "We're trying to help," I told her, even as she shook her head emphatically. "We're going to go to Nom."

The tiny body in front of me jerked in surprise, looking down at her tiny feet. They were gone, and whatever had erased them was working its way up her small form. She fixed a terrified green gaze on me and rounded her lips again. Then she repeated her previous request. "Help him!" and disappeared in a tiny pop of air.

A soft gasp sounded behind me. I turned to find Sebille standing about ten feet away, a book drooping from her fingers. "She's..."

I tensed, turning to my friend. "She wants us to help Jacob."

Sebille blinked in surprise. "She does?"

I pushed doubt away, thinking Sebille's shock was interesting. "Well yeah. It makes sense, right? We're just trying to save them."

Sebille's confused green gaze slid slowly toward mine. "You've met my mother, right?"

I frowned.

"She would never want us to give Jacob Quilleran the rune key."

My frown deepened. "If you believe that, then why are you so determined to do this?"

She rolled her eyes and I relaxed, realizing Sebille was okay. "I'm not going to let her die, Naida." The matter-of-fact way she stated the fact only confused me more. "So, you're willing to risk making her mad?"

Blowing air through her lips, Sebille said, "Have you met *me*?"

Giving up on the nonsensical conversation, I nodded at the book she held. "What did you find?"

"What?" Sebille dragged her gaze from the spot where her mother had appeared. "Oh, yeah. The book." Holding it up for me to see, she said. "I found the artifact we need."

"Great!"

It was her turn to frown.

"Not great?"

"No. That part's good. It's the part I haven't told you about yet that's bad."

I sighed. "Of course. Okay, hit me. What's the bad news?"

She lifted the book. "This says it's hidden in the Enchanted Forest."

I tensed again. "Oookay."

"Yeah." She winced. "It's in the cave of the wraiths."

I didn't respond. I couldn't. I was pretty sure the knot in my throat was going to end up choking me to death. "Are you sure?" I finally managed to choke out.

Sebille lifted the tome and showed me the picture and then closed it to show me the author of the book.

Doctor Mortimus Osvald, Professor of Devilry at the New York Institute of Magic.

I sighed. There'd been a time when Professor Osvald would have popped right up out of the book and nattered incessantly about whatever magical subject we were researching. Happily for him but annoying for our purposes, he was no longer cursed to live inside his prodigious writings.

"How detailed is the text on this artifact?" I asked the sprite.

Sebille shrugged. "Not detailed enough for us to throw ourselves into the path of a bunch of wraiths willy-nilly."

I dropped my head back and stared up at the ceiling, high, high above me. "I guess we're heading to the New York Institute of Magic to speak with Morty, then."

ONCE UPON A TIME...SEVERAL months earlier...we'd gone to the Enchanted Forest on a rescue mission to save my newly discovered brother from a powerful and besotted dual sorceress named Dacara. As punishment for an array of crimes, the sorceress had been banished to a castle on the mountainside in the Enchanted Forest. She couldn't leave the forest without some serious tom-foolery, but she *could* saturate the spot with deadly, disgusting wraiths that anyone dull enough to try to visit her castle would have to defeat before getting to her. Apparently, dull is my middle name because if we went again, it would be my third visit.

I shuddered, remembering my own experiences with the nasty creatures. I'd nearly died multiple times facing off against the things. In fact, I was pretty sure we'd all nearly died on that mountain.

And it looked as if we were going back.

I sighed long and loud, drawing Sebille's gaze to me. "What?"

"I'm praying Morty has a non-wraithy way to get hold of that artifact."

Sebille bounced up a step, her strides quick and light. I glanced her way and discovered she had a slight smile on her narrow, freckled face and her shimmery green gaze was even brighter than usual. She looked...happy. Despite the fact that everybody in the place was staring at her neon green skinny pants and apple-red tunic with splotches of yellow covering it. She looked like the love-child between a Christmas elf and Twiggy. Erg.

"Okay, what gives?"

"Hm?"

"Why aren't you cranky right now?"

She actually grinned. "Haven't you always wanted to visit the New York Institute of Magic?"

Her question caught me off guard. I'd never really thought about it. Granted, I'd come into my magic without any formal training, or really even any knowledge that it was going to happen...a long story featuring missing parents and a fake grandmother who was actually a troll...so there were many magical places I hadn't visited. But I'd never had any particular desire to visit the Institute.

I cast my gaze upward, to the enormous stone building that really looked more like a castle than a school, and felt my breath catch in my throat.

Since tumbling out of the Book of Pages in a stinky alley several moments earlier, I hadn't really looked at the famous school of magic. But once I looked...really looked... its awesome beauty finally hit me between the eyes. I jolted to a stop, my mouth hanging open. "Wow."

Sebille giggled. Yes. She actually giggled. "Amazing, right?"

The massive building perched high enough that clouds passed just above its spires. It sat on a rise of ground that spread flat and endless as far as the eye could see, defying the close-set brick and mortar aspect of the rest of the city. The steps we climbed appeared endless, climbing from street level to the base of the building above, which appeared to float upon the air, hanging high above the buildings around it.

Dense waves of flowers were everywhere on the grounds, bordering the wide stairs in the climb to the top, spilling over hundreds of huge concrete containers dotting the grounds, and lining every walkway spreading out across the vivid green grass.

The building itself was an aged brown, the blackened brick proclaiming its ancient status and the centuries of existence perched high above the streets of New York. In fact, it likely predated the city, and given its central location in Manhattan, had possibly already been there when non-magic humans began to build.

Before I knew it, we found ourselves at the top of the stairs. I'd expected to have to stop and rest at least once during the climb, but found instead that I had more energy than I'd had at the bottom.

Magic rose from the ground of the Institute. It swirled through the air and oozed from every brick that formed the building.

Magic infused every cell in my body and made me want to run and dance. It was addictive and intoxicating and I wanted more. It wasn't until Sebille poked me on the arm, the pain jerking me from my pleasure trance, that I realized how deeply I'd fallen beneath the Institute's spell.

I blinked, suddenly finding myself standing in an enormous lobby filled with people moving briskly to and fro. The floor beneath my feet was shiny black stone. The flecks of red and yellow infused in the stone sparkled under a solar-like output of light from the enormous crystal chandelier hanging from the high domical ceiling.

The lobby was encircled by two levels of white doors set into pale gray walls. A central staircase with curved banisters led upward to the second floor, the steps wider than I was tall. My gaze lifted to the upper balcony and I saw that the second level was just as busy as the first. People scurried from one place to the next, their hands and arms filled with papers, files, and books. Their steps were fast and light. Everyone inside the New York Institute of Magic seemed filled with a special purpose that I suddenly envied.

"Naida?"

I blinked, realizing I'd been lost to the magic again. "What?"

Sebille pointed to the stairs. "Morty's office is upstairs."

I nodded and followed, tripping once or twice on the steps as I gawked around instead of watching where I was going. I stepped onto the second level just as a door opened across from me and a tall young woman with coal black hair that fell past her narrow waist scurried out as if running from something. She nearly ran me over. Her cheeks pinkening, she apologized profusely and hurried on her way.

"It's this one," Sebille said.

I watched the young woman jog down the steps as if the hounds of Hell were nipping at her heels, wondering if she was under the influence of the building's magic, or if she was always that energetic.

"Naida! For the goddess's sake. Pay attention."

I spun around just as Sebille knocked on a door down the hall from where I stood.

"Come!" called a familiar, gruff voice from inside the office. Sebille opened the door and we stepped inside.

No matter how many times I laid eyes on Doctor Mortimus Osvald, the shock of seeing him as an entire body still made me twitch. For over a year, I'd known him only as a floating head that rose out of his books and served up snotty, though knowledgeable advice and information.

I'll admit he'd creeped me out a bit. There might have been a time or two when we'd slammed the books closed on his advice a tad harder than required. Then there was that one time Sebille had threatened to reinstate book burning in a literal sense. But somehow, we'd come through it all as almost friends.

It might have helped that he'd regained his form helping us ride a magical gas bubble called Altas Magnanimus. Alt-Mag for short. It turns out that when you get magically drunk...not sayin' I was...and then send Alt-Mag into a tail-spin trying to ram a snotty raven named Rasputin...long story...sometimes book heads turned into book bodies.

There's a slight chance that I made that more simplistic than it actually was. But you get the drift.

Osvald had been sitting behind the biggest desk I'd ever seen, but he stood when we walked in. From the neck up, he still looked like the floating head. That is to say, his dark brown hair was still scraggly. His ears still seemed too small for his head. And his complexion was still rough and ruddy as if he worked as a lumberjack flinging logs onto flatbeds, rather than a professor who flung nothing heavier than books.

As they had when he'd been inside his books, Osvald's black eyes still seemed to follow me wherever I went, often without turning his head very much. A side effect of being bodiless for so long? Probably.

Osvald's lips quirked slightly in his best imitation of a smile and the dense black eyebrows lowered, making him look like a comic book villain. "To what do I owe this great displeasure?" he said in a cultured British voice that seemed at odds with his rough exterior.

Sebille grinned in his direction. "Oy, Morty."

The man rolled his eyes at her Alice imitation. Alice Parker was the keeper who'd pretended to train me for my job as KoA. She was also British, but if I had to guess, not knowing anything about that part of the world, I'd say they'd probably grown up under different class labels. Of the two, Alice was generally more fun, though scatter-brained and a terrible cook.

"What can I do for you?" Professor Osvald tried again. "Believe it or not, I *am* a busy man."

"We've come to ask for your help." I gave him my best blank face, hoping my harmless demeanor might draw him into our web faster than Sebille's natural ability to annoy and offput. "We're looking for the book of glyphs that's hidden in the cave of the wraiths."

8

BING, BANG, BOB'S YOUR UNCLE!

Osvald stared at us for a long moment and then dropped into his chair, motioning toward the two chairs in front of his desk. "Sit. It appears we have much to discuss."

"Is the book really there?" I asked as I sat.

"Yes and no," he responded enigmatically. "The 'book' is actually a wall of glyphs." He frowned. "If you don't mind my asking, what do you need them for?"

Sebille and I shared a look. She frowned. I chewed my lip.

"Was that a difficult question?" Osvald asked.

"Yes," I admitted. "We're going on a rescue mission...of sorts." There. That wasn't a lie. Not really. Eventually we'd get to the rescue part. There was just a small, slightly illegal, wholly inadvisable part in the beginning which was giving us heartburn.

Osvald continued to stare at us from beneath those ridiculous brows. I forced myself to stop chewing my bottom lip and squared my shoulders. I refused to be the first one to break.

"Who exactly are you rescuing?" he asked.

"My mother," Sebille told him, her tone hostile. "And all the fairies."

Osvald's black eyes went round. "All of them?"

"Yes."

"Who took them?"

"Jacob Quilleran," I admitted. "So, you see, we need those glyphs. Can you just verify where they are for us and help us find a safe way to get them?"

He held up a hand. "Hold on. You speak as if it's just 'walk through the forest, take a left at the lake, duck into the caves and snatch up the book. Bing, bang, Bob's your uncle.'"

There it was. Apparently, Alice and Morty had more in common than I'd thought. "We know Bob's not our uncle," I said dryly. "That's why we came to you." His scary gaze narrowed on me as if trying to make sense of what I'd just said. He wasn't alone. I was trying to do the very same thing. "Anyway, can you help us with the glyphs?"

He shook his head, and angry heat flooded my cheeks.

"Why not?" Sebille asked.

Osvald leaned forward in his big leather chair and slid his gaze from me to the sprite. "Because you're not telling me the whole truth. Those glyphs lead to an artifact that copies objects down to the smallest nano particle. I can see no practical reason for you to need that type of thing in a rescue operation."

"We need to copy a key."

I glanced at Sebille, respect in my gaze. I inclined my chin slightly at her quick thinking. He didn't need to know what kind of key.

"What kind of key?"

A frustrated sigh burst free. "The rune key, okay? We need to copy the rune key," I admitted.

Sebille sucked air.

Morty slammed backward in his chair, his caterpillar-like brows riding his hairline. "Have you lost your minds?"

"No," Sebille said. "Which is why we're here. Jacob is demanding the key for the release of my mother and the fairies. We have no intention of giving him the rune key. But he doesn't need to know that."

Osvald sprang from his chair and started to pace the room, muttering to himself. He stopped and turned to us. "You do realize getting to the glyphs is nearly as dangerous as getting the rune key?"

I nodded without hesitation, though I hadn't realized that at all. My stomach churned with terror.

"If you have another suggestion, we're listening," Sebille said, her tone belligerent.

Osvald resumed pacing. He stopped again. "Is there no other way?"

Sebille filled him in on what Jacob had done to the fairies. He grew pale and then turned slightly gray. "Buffalo boogers," he finally breathed, dropping heavily into his chair. Clearly, he'd been hanging around us for too long. "So, you're going to copy the key and try to pass off the copy to Jacob?"

We nodded.

"He'll know right away the key doesn't hold the magic it should."

"We're going to feed it small amounts of every kind of magic we can come up with," I told him. "We just need to buy enough time to get the fairies free."

"Have you thought about going after Quilleran directly?"

"We have," I said. "But without him, it will be nearly impossible to save the queen and the fairies."

Osvald sprang from his chair again, and resumed pacing. He ran a hand over his jawline as he paced, the sound of whiskers against his palm peppering the air.

"Do you know a way to save them without him?" I asked, hope threading my voice.

Morty didn't respond, continuing to pace. As if he were operating under a time-delay, he shook his head a moment later. "No. But as a void master your uncle might."

"He's looking into it," Sebille said, shoulders rounded with worry.

Sighing, Morty dropped heavily into his chair. "I'll help you get to the glyphs, but it will be up to you at that point. I can't read them...well, at least not all of them. You'll need to decipher the glyphs to reach the replication artifact."

"Is there a guide to help us read them?" I asked.

Morty inclined his head. "I'll see what I can find. Now..." He pulled a lined tablet over in front of him. "Let's discuss options for getting to the cave safely and surviving the retrieval of the glyphs." He frowned. "It is my understanding that Dacara has tripled her wraith population since the last time we were there. We're not going to be able to just walk into that cave. We'll be dead before we get three feet inside."

I blinked. "You're coming with us?"

"Of course." He looked as surprised as I felt. "I feel responsible, since you did find the artifact through one of my reference volumes." He picked up a pen and started scribbling. "This is what I think we should do."

～

I LEANED against the rocky surface and panted. My muscles quivered violently and I had to lock my knees to keep from plunging into the valley below. My sweat molecules had sweat molecules of their own. I pried a thick ribbon of my long brown hair off my wet face and shoved it back, my tongue hanging out of my mouth as I tried to pull air into my overtaxed lungs.

Next to me, Sebille arched a brow, then sent a meaningful glance downward, to the wide flat shelf of rock where Birte waited in all her dragonly glory, a mere fifteen feet below us. Granted, she was under a cloaking spell that just made her look like slightly shiny air, but I knew she was there.

I scowled at the sprite. "I'm not in shape for rock climbing," I growled out. "Sue me."

"You've climbed fifteen feet and it's not even very steep."

"Come on, ladies," Osvald whisper-shouted ahead of us. "We need to get in and out of here before darkness falls."

His reminder had my spongy arms reaching for a nearby scrub tree to pull my marshmallow legs another foot higher. "Why..." I panted before sucking in another gulp of air. "...couldn't whoever hid these glyphs..." I sucked in another lungful as I fought my way another foot higher. "...have hidden them in a lower cave?"

Sebille burst into her sprite form and buzzed near my eye-level, hands on hips. "Gee, I don't know, Naida," she said, her snot-o-meter in full disdain mode. "Maybe they didn't want just anybody to access a dangerous artifact."

Dangerous. Yeah. I needed to keep reminding myself of that. With the replication artifact in hand, someone like Jacob Quilleran could create no end of havoc.

She buzzed skyward, easily bypassing the muscle-busting forty-five-degree climb to the cave above. "Jerk!" I called after her, inspiring a gleeful titter that floated mockingly down the mountain in my direction.

A chilly breeze slipped over me, the stench of wraith filling my nostrils and kicking my pulse into overdrive. The rocky outcrop I was reaching for felt slimier than it should have, and my fingers slipped, leaving me windmilling for balance twenty feet above the hard shelf where our ride waited.

Birte belched out a thick burst of fire which heated the air just behind me. I tightened my soft underbelly and yelped, my hand somehow finding a fingerhold as I scrambled upward in panic.

Above me, Sebille and Morty disappeared from sight as they moved away from the edge toward the cave.

I scrambled faster and, a few minutes later, finally stepped onto the path through the woods that I really hoped led to the cave. My legs wobbled dangerously and I bent double, my lungs hee-hawing like a donkey as I fought for air.

One of these days, I really needed to get into better shape.

Probably not one of these days soon, though.

I came upon the yawning blackness of the cave face thirty yards away. Taking a deep breath, I stepped into the unnatural blackness. "Sebille? Morty?" My whisper sounded too loud in the silence and I cringed. As I stepped into the blustery darkness from the heat of the dying sun, the damp cold of the place hit me like a slap to the face.

I blinked around, trying to adjust my eyesight to the new low-level illumination. Something shadowy moved in my periphery and I yelped, dodging sideways. Morty's ugly mug emerged from the shadows, a disembodied horror that was only marginally less terrifying than the wraiths we were trying to avoid. "Goddess in a gondola," I breathed out, clapping a hand over my pounding heart. "You scared the beans out of me."

"This way," Osvald said, his voice a dry rasp in the silence.

"Did you find them?" I asked hopefully. Maybe we *could* make quick work of the glyphs, grab the artifact, and skedaddle back to our waiting dragon. Bing, bang, Bob's your uncle.

Morty's derisive huff told me I was being way too optimistic.

A light flickered on and Osvald shone it on an icy cave wall several feet away. As the light swam over the rockface, I saw the opening to a passageway cutting through the rock. "That way," he said, twitching the flashlight over the opening.

We both stood there for a beat. If I could have seen his expression, I expect I'd have been looking at a pointedly arched caterpillar or two.

Finally, I said, "You should go first. You have the flashlight."

He nodded, but instead of stepping forward, he reached down and grabbed my hand, smacking the flashlight into my palm.

I started forward on a sigh, reminding myself he was there to help us. It was our mission. There was no need for him to endanger himself unnecessarily. The rationalization made sense. But it didn't keep me from throwing him a glare before setting off at a too-slow pace to find Sebille.

The sprite was a distance away, down the passage. Her fairy light flickered over the walls as she buzzed slowly along, searching for glyphs. I hurried to catch up, Osvald's big feet clomping along behind me.

The sprite's light disappeared and the passage ahead went dark. My heart skipped a beat and my footsteps faltered. I stopped short. Morty slammed into me, my hands shot up protectively as I hit the wall. The flashlight hit the ground, skittering across the rocky dirt and going dark.

We stood in expectant silence, the only sound the babump, babump, babump of our hearts. Morty's clothing rustled as he moved closer, his breath scalding the back of my neck.

I opened my mouth to ask him if he'd seen where the flashlight landed, but something swished past over our heads. The stench of the grave wafted over us, and a chill sank deep into my bones. Something touched my face and I jolted, biting down on the scream trying to crawl its way out of my throat.

Orange eyes glowed through the velvety darkness.

Wraiths.

The darkness was thick and sharp, its edges only occasionally softened by the passage of unadulterated evil. An oily feeling of dread turned my chest to ice. I was sweating and shaking with fear at the same time. Something that felt like claws clamped onto my shoulder and I gave a short, sharp scream. A hand slapped over my mouth and Osvald leaned in, his hot breath bathing my ear as he whispered. "We need to stay perfectly still and silent."

No duh! It would probably help if he didn't startle me into screaming. I nodded and we slowly melted backward, keeping as small a profile as possible as what felt like an army of the nasty creatures floated past.

A few very long minutes later, the soft buzz of Sebille's wings approached. They stopped mere inches from my face, whacking me on the nose. I fought the desire to swat at her like a large, annoying bug. "Come on, Naida. We're losing daylight."

Speaking of light. "I dropped the flashlight. Can you give us a little illumination?"

She rubbed her iridescent purple and green butterfly wings and a soft whir created a gentle glow of pale green light. I found the flash a few feet away and snatched it up.

"Let's just go by my light for a while," Sebille suggested. "In case another group of wraiths decides to wander by."

"Good idea," I murmured.

We started off again, my body still giving in to the occasional violent shiver as I tried to cast abject fear aside. We just needed to find the glyphs and get the artifact. Then we could go home. I kept repeating that in my mind as my eyes scoured the walls, searching for the symbols we needed along their icy lengths.

We entered a larger space, a cavern by the feel of it. Sound played back to me in small echoes. Our footfalls bounced around and reverberated unnervingly. Sebille's faint light was swallowed into the space and the slightly claustrophobic feeling from the passageway was gone.

Sebille rose up along the wall, toward a ceiling that was so high above us and so dark we couldn't see it. Shadows ate away at our vision, cloaking the vast space around us and creating a living nightmare that was low on visibility but high on the sour stench of death.

Judging by the smell, we'd wandered into a place where the wraiths spent a lot of time.

"We need to do this fast," Osvald said. His voice was raspy and harsh, his movements jittery. The man was clearly as spooked as I was.

I turned on the flashlight and started down a wall. Sebille flew to an adjacent wall and we began our search in earnest. I found what we were looking for several minutes later, as the main wall I'd been following dipped into a small alcove. As soon as my light skidded over the alcove walls, I saw them. Dark etchings danced in uneven rows across the cranny, continuing around the curves in the walls and dropping down to start again when the wall space ended.

I stuck my head out of the alcove, speaking barely above a whisper. "Here!"

I immediately went to work, trying to read the strange whirls and slashes and even the occasional stick person or creature with horns and tails that were supposed to tell us a story. It was a story I wasn't understanding. The more I tried to read the glyphs, the more their meaning skittered away from me.

In my mind's eye, I visualized the sun dipping below the horizon outside. I pictured a hundred wraiths roaring from the cave to poison the night beyond.

I shuddered at the thought of being caught within that mass of death and horror.

Sebille buzzed into the alcove and spun around, trying to read the glyphs. "These make no sense," she said a moment later.

Hovering over a particularly impossible string of symbols, she pointed to what looked like a stick woman wearing a long gown and standing next to what could only be considered a picnic table, which held a single arrow on its surface. Next to the table was one of the horned creatures, its eyes slitted and its jagged teeth on display.

From that string, dancing off to either side, were a series of symbols that looked like musical notes mixed with ancient Roman numerals. Another arrow divided those icons from a group of stick figures with strange, oval hair and long gowns, whose centers bore long slashes as if someone had cut into them.

"Gruesome," I muttered. On the ground around the women were more of the strange arrows.

"Wait," Morty said. He pointed to the stick women. "That isn't hair. They're hoods. And those..."

As he pointed to the gashes part of the puzzle fell into place. "They're wraiths." When we'd fought the wraiths before, the center of their spider-like forms split apart in about a ten-inch vertical slash to emit a thick, silvery mist that ate away human skin and any magic barriers we'd tried to create.

"Life centers," Sebille said, hovering nearby.

"Yes," Morty said, nodding excitedly. He pointed to the picnic table. "Food." Then to the group of wraiths. "Social." Then his long finger found a glyph I'd really struggled with. It looked like a bunch of bats hanging upside down. "Maybe this means cave?" He shook his head.

"So, it's in this cave. We already knew that, right?" Sebille said, sounding frustrated.

We all stared at the symbols for another minute. I was vaguely aware of a distant soft swishing noise that might have been from bats.

I ran my gaze over the entire thing, top to bottom, and finally spotted the pattern. "Arrows."

"Huh?" Sebille said.

I hurried forward, playing the light over an arrowhead I'd initially assumed was a random triangle. "See, here's the head." I slid my fingers along the shaft, outlined by more arrow icons, to the "feathers". When I looked at it as a whole rather than individual shapes, I realized they all encircled that main arrow.

We slowly turned and looked out into the cavern. I

shone my light along the floor, walking quickly, and found what I was looking for carved into a large plank of rock buried in the center. The carving formed a perfect circle, consisting of hundreds of etched arrows. And at its center, encircled by all the arrowheads, was a perfect round area made of a chalky black substance.

The artifact.

"We found it!" My voice echoed throughout the cavern and I slapped my hand over my mouth. We listened through a beat of silence and, just when I thought it was going to be okay, a piercing scream shattered the silence and an explosion of shadows burst away from the ceiling, diving straight for us.

Wraiths!

9

ACTIVATING FLYING SNEAKERS NOW

ak! The wraiths had been hanging from the ceiling like bats. The first shriek set off a cacophony of screams and screeches which brought us to our knees, our hands covering our ears. The sound was terrifying. Debilitating. But we couldn't afford to stay there. We had to move. We needed to get the artifact and hightail it out of there.

The sprite threw two handfuls of neon green dust at me and it sifted over my head, blissfully dulling the wraiths' deadly screams. "Get the artifact!" Sebille yelled, before throwing more dust on Osvald.

I tugged a zipper bag from my pocket and dropped to my knees, my gaze continually sliding upward as thousands of glowing orange eyes lit the air above. A putrid-smelling figure slashed past me, catching in my hair and tugging painfully as it kept on going.

I ducked lower, my heart pounding as I dug into the chalky substance in the center of the carving and scooped a handful into the bag. I'd just managed to scoop a second handful when something slammed into me, its weight driving me to the ground.

Claws scraped over my shoulder, agony slicing through the dulling mask of fear. It yanked a scream from my throat before I could stop myself. Not that it mattered anyway. The cavern was thick with screams. Mine just merged with all the rest.

"We need to go," Morty yelled into my sound-dampened ears. I realized with a start that it had been him who'd slammed into me. Had he thrown himself on top of me to stop the wraith from doing it first?

I looked down at the black substance. "I need more."

He shook his head, leaped to his feet more agilely than I would ever have suspected he was capable of, and grabbed my arm, wrenching me to my feet. "We have to go. Now!"

I let him yank me away, casting a final, wistful glance back at the nearly unspoiled cache of replicating carbon, and then quickly zipped my bag before I lost what little I'd gathered.

A spine-melting shriek sounded directly above me and fear made me stumble. Ice climbed through the air and smacked into me, turning my limbs to frozen rubber.

The wraith shot past mere inches above my head, its orange eyes glowing with feral glee.

But it didn't attack.

"It's working," I told Osvald as we headed toward Sebille. The sprite's tiny form hovered near the cavern entrance to the passageway. She was shooting bursts of magic through the cavern to discombobulate and distract the wraiths, giving Morty and I the only cover we could manage.

Osvald nodded at me, flashing me a brief smile. He twitched in alarm at something he saw behind me, the whites of his eyes glowing in the residue from Sebille's magical light show.

"Down!" he screamed.

I hit the hard ground with an "Umph!" and he landed next to me.

My heart slammed against my ribs. My lungs fought for air as the combination of fear and too much exercise over-taxed them.

The shadowy form of an enormous wraith moved toward us, flying low. Its claws trailed along the ground as if it knew we were there. I turned my head enough to see it hesitate just above us, the frigid cold of the grave coating the entire area around the massive creature. I watched in horror as the center of its spidery body slit open, something molten and silver roiling within the orifice.

I clamped a hand on Osvald. "Morty!" I whispered.

His eyes were like saucers in his chalky face. "I..."

There was nothing he could do. His magic was book-related. Unless he could whip out a book of bedtime stories and lull the monster to sleep, he was useless.

But so was I. My magic would do little to harm the wraith. Actually, any energy we hit it with would only strengthen it. That was one of the challenges of battling wraiths, and the reason Sebille was using her magic as a distraction rather than a weapon.

The only weapon we had was the miniaturized Book of Pages in my pocket, but I'd never manage the process of using it under the current circumstances, and we couldn't leave Sebille behind anyway, so that idea was a non-starter.

Right on cue, the sprite speared the air inches above the wraith with a bolt of energy. Her bolt passed by so closely, the edge of the thing's empty hood sizzled with magic for a beat before dulling again.

Unfortunately, it did nothing to scare the wraith away. It was easily the biggest wraith I'd ever seen, which probably meant it was more powerful than the others.

Wraith wrinkles!

Meanwhile, back at the wraith's unfortunately located "mouth", stuff was about to spew.

I didn't intend to be around when it happened.

"Roll!" I said, squeezing Osvald's arm. To his credit, he rolled. I was right behind him. By the time the acidic spew hit the ground beneath the wraith, Sebille was blasting head-sized holes into the ground all around it. The thing was so distracted by the eruptions, it didn't seem to notice Osvald and I were gone.

As soon as we were out of the line of fire, we took off running. We hit the passageway hard, moving fast. Sebille peppered the cavern with a series of final blasts and then shot past us up the passage.

The corridor was dark, but not quite as dark as the cavern had been. Still, after several moments of running, I started to worry. We should have been seeing some light from the entrance by that point.

It took only another minute to realize why we weren't.

No light filtered in through the entrance when we reached it. Darkness had fallen. The blackness we plunged into when we left the cave was as dark as the passageway had been. And chock full of hungry wraiths.

Frog flatulence!

Sebille buzzed back to us. "We have to get to the dragon," she said. "You need to make like a wraith or you're not going to get there."

I held my hands out to show her my wispy black robe. Beneath the hood, my face was blackened and I had small round lights stuck to my cheeks below my eyes, they glowed orange like the wraiths' eyes did. I tried not to think about the stink spell Sebille had coated us with that made us smell like wraiths too. "This has worked so far."

She shook her head. "In an enclosed space. But out here, nobody's on the ground. If you don't get airborne, they're going to know you're not one of them."

I winced. It had been my idea to wear sneakers that were bespelled to act like flying carpets, but we hadn't had time to practice with them and I had a strong feeling my sneaker-fueled flight was not going to be pretty. "Maybe if we stuck close to the rocks..."

"Use the sneakers, Naida," Sebille barked. "I'm going to try to lead them away. If you get into trouble use the wraith whistle I gave you. It disorients them. But once you use it, they'll know where you are so don't go crazy with it."

I rolled my eyes at her but she couldn't see it in the dark. "We'll be fine." I only wished I felt half as confident as I sounded.

"She's right, Naida." Morty's gaze skimmed over the sky, drawing my gaze upward. I gasped. The night was full of the nasty creatures. Hundreds of them, like giant blood-sucking bats, blackened the gray sky above. I swallowed hard. "Activating flying sneakers now."

Sebille flew off as I bent down and touched my finger to the glistening spot on the toe of the first shoe. It came on with a hiss and that leg jerked upward before I could engage the second one. "Ah!" My leg whipped out and nailed Osvald in the side.

"Ow!" He shot skyward before I could apologize, disappearing inside the branches of a massive tree. One knee up around my waist, I tracked his passage through the tree by the sound of each branch he careened into and the groans of pain that followed.

I tried to shove the knee of my activated leg down so I could reach my second shoe but it sprang back up and clocked me in the eye. "Bungie jumping Basset Hound!" I exclaimed before I caught myself and checked the nearest wraiths. Several pairs of glowing eyes had turned my way.

Oops.

I lunged toward my earthbound shoe and missed, grunting as my fluffy middle was overly compressed by the effort.

A distant scream had my head shooting up.

Several wraiths were coming my way to investigate. Apparently, they'd never seen a badly dressed wraith with googly orange eyes trying to bend down and touch her shoe with one knee jammed into her armpit.

Frog snot!

A second wraith screamed and they came faster, anticipating a victim.

Magic blasted dirt and rock into the air in their flight path but it barely slowed them. I needed to get out of there, and fast.

I flung myself to the ground and slammed my palm onto the earthbound sneaker. It came on with a hiss and I lifted off the ground, then shot backward, my head and shoulders slamming into the grassy rise behind me.

Pain shot down my neck and I bounced off the rise, only to slam into it again as my shoes tried to get me off the ground,

Groaning, I pushed myself into a more or less vertical position and shoved hard on the grass. I shot skyward.

Sort of.

I was heading for the rock face above at an impossible speed. Frantically swinging my arms, I tried to right myself. But control was a distant goal. All my flailing did was send me into spirals on the air. The world around me spun so fast it made me dizzy and I had to close my eyes. Which turned out to be a good thing, because I was heading for the same tree that had attacked Morty.

It was probably best if I didn't watch my death coming at me.

I slammed up against something hard and rough, wrapping my arms around the tree trunk and holding on while I wheezed in an effort to regain the breath that had been knocked out of me.

The tree swayed slightly and bits of leaf and sticks rained down on me. The soft whir of magic sneakers made its way past the terror thudding in my mind. "Stay there," Morty said, sounding every bit as breathless as me. "Maybe they won't see us here."

Magic slammed into the tree, the concussion making it sway violently as branches splintered around us.

"Sebille!" I said, wrapping myself around the tree like a monkey. I hung on, having no other choice, while the shoes kept smacking my knees into the underside of the branch below me.

We waited and listened, but there were no more blood-curdling shrieks. None of the wraiths came searching for us in the tree.

Sebille's unfortunate and ill-advised blast of energy had apparently driven them away. That, of course, didn't mean I wasn't going to wrap my fingers around her throat and squeeze once we got out of there.

"I think we can go now," Morty whispered.

I shook my head. "The last thing I want to do is let go of this tree."

Whomp, my knee hit the branch. *Whomp*.

"We just need to straighten up, point our bodies in the

right direction, and not wiggle or twitch," Morty said, the voice of delusional experience.

I sighed. I knew he was right Birte wouldn't wait there forever.

"Take my hand," Morty said.

I glanced over and saw his offered hand. I frowned. "I don't think you want to tether yourself to me. I'm like a runaway train on a corkscrew track."

He didn't smile or try to deny it. I'll admit, it was a little hurtful. "But, you're going to do better now. Right?" He narrowed his black eyes on me.

I sighed. "I'll try."

I clasped his hand and found a solid branch with my feet. Then I slowly turned, one arm still wrapped around a branch to keep me from premature launch.

I straightened as much as I could and pulled air into my lungs.

"Ready?"

I shook my head. But slowly released the branch.

Whoosh! We jerked skyward and, with only a few small branches in the face, we were off.

10

OUR PLAN IS MISSION IMPLAUSIBLE

"You have a little something..." Sebille pointed to my teeth. "Right there."

I plucked a piece of leaf out of my teeth, glowering at her. "Thanks for blowing up the tree we were in."

She grinned. "You're welcome."

Behind us, Birte shifted uneasily, her massive silver frame taking up most of the wide shelf we were standing on. *Those wraiths are going to find us if we don't leave soon.*

Recognizing Birte's husky voice in my head, I turned to her and nodded. "I know. We're ready."

A not-too-distant shriek filled the air in the direction we'd just come from. The wraiths were heading our way fast. "Come on," I told Osvald.

"You don't have to tell me twice," he grumbled, limping toward the dragon.

I limped after him, twinges in my battered thighs making me twitch and shamble like a zombie.

The sprite tittered behind me. When I cast a glare in her direction, she laughed. "I don't know why you're mad at me for exploding that tree, you've done more than enough damage to yourself taking off and landing in those shoes."

She wasn't wrong. If my takeoff in the goddess-be-darned shoes had been ugly, it had been nothing compared to my crash landing in them. As if responding to her mirth, the shoes gave off several small bursts of air that had me ugly-dancing my way toward Birte.

The gorgeous silver dragon snorted out some smoke, her hilarity rumbling like a forest fire inside her chest.

"Ha," I told the two of them. "Let's just get out of here. Morty and I want to have a shoe-burning ceremony in the quad."

"The New York Institute of Magic does not have a *quad*," he sneered arrogantly.

I shrugged. "Then we'll burn them in the street. I don't really care." My unrepentant footwear gave a last little burst that blew me into Birte and then went quiet.

"Stupid shoes."

I was barely astride the dragon's long, scaly back when she swung around in apparent alarm. She opened her elegant snout and sent a wall of fire into the sky. Behind the fire, several terrifying screams rent the air.

"We need to go!" Sebille screamed. She shot into the air and sent a barrage of magic into the ground beneath the approaching mass of wraiths. Dust, grass and rock flew upward, slamming into the glowy-eyed monsters and doing nothing to slow or stop them.

Birte sent another wave of fire into them and then pointed her nose skyward. She gave one good pound of her wings before they were on us. Several wraiths burst through the fiery barrier and they were on top of us before I even had time to scream.

Claws dug into my arms, slamming me flat against Birte.

A putrid mass of death and horror hovered over me, its empty hood with the glowing eyes inches from my face. An unfathomable cold swept through me, locking my limbs and freezing my insides.

Horrific images of death and terror slipped through my mind, the reflections of my most devastating fears crisp in their presentation and sharp enough to cut.

My screams melded with Morty's and Birte's. In that moment, I knew we would die. I saw our deaths in crystal-clear depictions that were indiscernible from reality.

My throat burned from screaming. My heart galloped in my chest. I was so cold I was certain I'd chipped a few teeth from the violence of their chattering. But worse than my own plight was the predicament of the beautiful creature beneath me. Birte's cries were heartbreaking and I could only imagine what horrors the wraiths were showing her.

"Void...?" I gritted out between screams. I wasn't sure the word had really even emerged. My throat was so raw it was hard to speak. The last time we'd been confronted by the nasty things, Uncle Archie had used voids to rid us of them.

It was the only kind of magic I knew of that could save us. Though I was pretty sure none of the people I was with could create a void.

Whistle! The single word slammed into my mind and my hand moved. I'd added a little pocket in my wraith robe to hide it in, so it would be easy to grab. Terrible images pummeled me. The cold was relentless, my limbs stiff from it. For a moment I forgot what I was trying to do, and when I remembered I couldn't bend my fingers enough to grab the whistle.

"Sebille," I tried again, shoving at the wraith poisoning my thoughts with more strength than I would have expected. When I tried to focus on the sprite, I became aware of bursts of magical energy around us, and realized Sebille was fighting her own personal battle. I reached blindly for Osvald. "Help!" The request was desperate, filled with despair.

His icy hand touched mine and he gave my fingers a feeble squeeze. "Book," he said. Like my voice, his was raw and the word was little more than a whisper.

I shook my head. Books were his thing. But I didn't see how they could help...

Then it hit me. I understood what he was telling me. We couldn't shoot magic at the wraiths because they absorbed whatever we hit them with and just grew stronger. But we could use non-defensive magic against them. And the Book of Pages was just the ticket.

I fought to get to the miniaturized book in my pocket, but the wraith was in the way. The first time I touched its cold, mushy form I shuddered hard enough to crack a tooth. My muscles were heavy and uncooperative, and my fingers were numb.

A fresh spate of nightmares flitted through my mind. Death, terror, hopelessness. I was too tired and cold to even scream. My vision had grayed out and my eyes were so heavy I just wanted to sleep. Just a few hours of rest...

The world lit up in vibrant hues as heat washed over me. The wraith clinging to my body shot away. It hung in the air above me, writhing and shrieking like it was on fire. An enormous set of jaws were wrapped around it.

"It can't be," I murmured as the wraith was wrenched in two and flung carelessly away.

The chimera!

I stared at the mythical creature in front of me with my mouth hanging open. The chimera was easily twice as tall as my five feet nine inches. Its wings were massive, as they'd have to be to carry the enormous creature through the air. The living myth moved closer, smoke wafting in fragrant streams from its leonine nose. The nostrils flared and a hollow chuff sounded, the thick golden mane quivering with interest. The eyes were golden too. They were intelligent eyes, but not in any way human.

The thing's leathery dragon wings had curved claws at the apex of their bony frames, and its paws sported long, deadly-looking claws that could rip a human apart with a single blow. His tail was thicker than a lion's but had the same general shape, with a ball of fur on the end like the big cat's.

A pile of torn and unmoving wraiths lay at his feet.

Sebille buzzed up to me and landed on Birte's quivering shoulder. "It's okay, Birte. That's Rustin. He won't..."

With a roar, the dragon shot off the ground, dumping Osvald and me unceremoniously to the ground, and shot away like the hounds of Hades were on her tail.

"Ugh," I groaned, shoving back to a seated position. "I'm pretty tired of being flung around and bludgeoned."

"Ditto," groaned Morty. His gaze landed on Rustin and lit with an excited glow. "But it's all worth it to see this. The legendary chimera." He shook his head. "Stupendous."

The thing that was Rustin moved closer. His steps were ponderous in the relatively small space of the rock shelf. The ground rumbled with every step and I started to worry that the shelf wouldn't hold beneath his bulk. On the tail end of that thought, dirt and rock tumbled down from above and pinged off into the abyss. The chimera's nostrils flared again, his leonine head stretching closer as if to scent us. He threw back his head and roared again. Morty and I flinched but held our ground.

After a beat, light and heat flashed and Rustin stood

before us. We stared at each other for a minute and then I sighed. "Thanks for the rescue. How'd you find us?"

He shook his head, still looking angry. "Later." He jerked his head toward the castle in the distance. "If you don't want to fight another wave of those things, we should probably get out of here."

RUSTIN and I sat at the table in a darkened Croakies. Mr. Wicked was sitting in my lap, purring, and Vel was in Rustin's lap. The little demon dog was snoring softly, clearly up past her bedtime. Rustin ran his fingers through Vel's soft green fur, his expression thoughtful.

We were both exhausted. Him from shifting several times within a short time frame and then flying Osvald and me home, and me from...well...everything.

But for me, at least, it was a contented weariness. We'd managed to accomplish the first step in our journey to save the fairies. It had been ugly. But we'd survived.

I lifted my gaze to him as he sipped his tea. "Thank you for showing up. We probably wouldn't have made it out if you hadn't. I still can't believe you found us."

"Lea called me. She begged me to help."

"Thank the goddess she did."

He nodded, then frowned. "Naida, this is crazy. You know that, right?"

Expelling air in a heartfelt sigh, I said, "Yep." I caught his gaze and held it. "We can't just leave the fairies there," I told him. "And there's something you're not considering. If we don't do this, he'll move on to someone else, threaten their loved ones, and force them to get the key. Jacob Quilleran likes to get what he wants. You, of all people should understand that."

He nodded again, pursing his lips. In the dim light, with his dark hair disheveled and his wire rimmed glasses missing, he looked slightly dangerous, his strong jaw, perfect nose, and full lips making him look like a storybook hero. But he looked older too, despite the fact that he was only a few years older than me. In that moment I realized just how much Rustin had gone through in his short life. Most of it because of Jacob Quilleran. "Yeah," he finally said. "I know what Uncle Jacob is capable of." He leaned forward, putting his elbows on the table. He fixed me with an intense gaze as Vel rearranged herself in his lap, yawning widely. "I'm sorry I got mad. I know you're doing what you need to do. If I'd been with you today..."

I reached out and grabbed his hand, squeezing it. "You were there when we needed you. No regrets, Rustin. Don't let Jacob take any more of your life by getting into your head. He's a ruthless derf and everything that happens to us during this mission is his fault. Not yours. Not mine. His."

He squeezed my hand. "You're right."

We fell into silence again. A moment later, he said, "Knowing my uncle as I do, I have to tell you something."

"Okay." I sipped my tea too, closing my eyes as heat slid through me. I was still cold from my wraith experience. In fact, I felt as if I'd never be warm again.

"It's not like him to send somebody else in for the key, Naida. It feels off somehow."

I'd had a similar thought. "You think he's setting us up?"

"No. I can't think of anything he'd gain from that. But something's wrong with this mission. I can feel it in my bones."

I laughed, earning a surprised glance from him. "Sorry.

But everything's wrong with this mission. It's a cluster farce waiting to happen. Our plan is Mission Implausible. We're doomed to failure." I drifted off, all humor sliding away. Tears burned my eyes. "But I can't tell Sebille we're leaving her mother behind." I ran a hand under my eyes. "I just can't do it."

"I know." Rustin smiled tightly. "That's why I'm on board for the rest of this mission."

I sniffed. "Really?"

"Really." He lowered Vel gently to the floor and stood up. "I'm going home. Sadie needs to be fed and let out for some exercise." Sadie was Rustin's amalgamate dragon, a tiny, rare creature from the rainforests of Hawaii. Rustin opened the door and looked back at me. "I'll see you in the morning?"

"Bright and early," I said, smiling. "Thanks again, Rustin." I watched him leave and then dragged my weary body into a standing position, shambling over to set the locks and wards on Croakies' front door. I was sore and tired. I felt a million years old as I opened the dividing door to head upstairs to my apartment.

I jumped back with a soft yelp as two whirling dervishes shot through the door into the bookstore.

Baca and Hobs flashed around the room giggling happily.

I smiled at their antics, enjoying the moment of normalcy. "Night guys," I called out, getting a chorus of responses back from the pair. "See you in the morning."

11

HERE COMES DA FROG

"Have you made any progress in the search for Queen Sindra and the fairies?" I asked my uncle.

Archie frowned. "Not really. I've isolated potential locations down to a thousand or so possibilities. But whittling it from there is going to be difficult."

"What parameters are you using?" Grym asked the void sorcerer.

Flicking him a look, Archie sighed. "That's the problem. The parameters are broad. I don't know enough about their situation to narrow them. Their state of suspended demolecularization can only be achieved under certain conditions. If we factor in the ability to remolecularize, that narrows it down further."

"How much further?" Sebille asked.

Archie seemed reluctant to say, but he finally responded with, "To about a hundred void areas."

"That's not bad," Sebille said, hope shining in her bright green gaze.

Archie looked down at his notebook, which was filled

with squiggles and scratches only he could decipher. He didn't seem to want to meet the sprite's gaze.

"What are you thinking?" I asked him.

He shook his head.

"Please," I asked. "If it's possible to locate them, we won't need to get the rune key."

With a flicker of a glance at Sebille, he finally said. "I'm just not sure we can assume Jacob was telling the truth about getting the fairies back."

Sebille glowered at him.

He lifted his hands. "I'm sorry, Sebille. You know I'll keep looking. But it might be a fool's errand to assume they're in a place where they can be retrieved."

What he wasn't saying was that, in all probability, they were beyond help.

I shook my head, refusing to follow his line of reasoning. "We have to work toward the assumption we can get them back." I risked a look at the sprite, whose eyes were hard with anger. "Remember, Sindra was able to appear briefly to us. They're out there and they're waiting for us to find them. Use the remolecular-whatever factor and reduce the possibilities as much as you can. As soon as you figure out where they are, get word to us. We're going to move forward with our plan to invade the vault on Nom."

He nodded, still unable to meet Sebille's gaze. I hadn't convinced him. But he'd do as I asked. I just prayed he'd find them before we all found death or imprisonment on Nom.

"You've got the drawings of the vault?" Rustin asked Archie.

He nodded. "Unfortunately, there were no depictions of the inside. You'll have to get through the front door first."

I grimaced, my stomach twisting at the idea.

"The lock isn't anything special," Archie went on. "The door is reinforced steel. But the real problem is the Nomook."

"Nomook?" Lea asked, frowning. "I've never heard of that. What is it?"

"You wouldn't have," Archie said. "It's part of a Nomish myth from millennia ago, when the realm was still populated. Think of a Cerberus, but..." He glanced at Wicked, who was playfully chasing a puff of lint across the floor. "It's feline instead of canine."

My eyes widened. "Seriously? A three-headed cat?"

Archie inclined his head. "By all accounts, a truly magnificent beast. I only wish I was going to be there to see it."

"My chimera can take care of it," Rustin said.

"No!" Archie said, looking horrified. "You can't kill it. You can't kill any of the guardians of the vault. To do so would ensure that you'd spend the rest of your days in prison. The only way we gain a measure of forgiveness for this misadventure is to create as little harm as possible."

I knew he was right. But that made what we were about to do twice as difficult as it already was. My stomach churned with worry. I tried to keep it out of my expression, but realized I hadn't been successful when Grym reached out and squeezed my hand.

"Any ideas how to get past the Nomook without hurting it?" my boyfriend asked.

A thought flitted through my mind and I smiled. "Actually, I might have just the thing."

"Good," Lea said. She turned to my uncle. "Archie, I know you couldn't get pictures or blueprints, but do you have any idea what's inside the vault? What besides the Nomook are we going to come up against?"

He sighed. "The Universal Council designed the vault to be impermeable. The first level of protection is the fact that there's no physical way to get to Nom." He nodded at me. "But I think we have that covered. Next is the triple moons."

"Triple moons?" Sebille asked.

"Yes," Archie said. "The vault cannot be accessed unless the three moons of Nom are full and in complete alignment."

"When is that due to happen again?" Grym asked.

"Those calculations are complex," Archie told him. "I've got someone working on them."

"Wait. Who?" I asked. "You told somebody what we're doing?"

"Isn't that dangerous?" Rustin asked.

Archie held up a perfectly manicured hand. "Don't worry. It's just my assistant. She believes it's research for a paper I'm writing. It will be fine." He crossed his arms over his chest. "We've already discussed the Nomook. The next hurdle is the magician."

"What's his name," I asked.

Archie looked at me as if I had three heads like the Nomook. "What difference does that make?"

"If we need to convince him to help us, it would be good to have his name."

Archie snorted a laugh. "The young are so optimistic. The magician's name is the least of your worries. Besides, it's unknown."

"What's his trick?" I asked.

"Trivia," Archie said.

Silence pulsed through the room.

I opened my mouth and then slammed it shut. Even Sebille seemed at a loss. Wouldn't it be ironic if something as mundane as a trivia-spouting magician was our undoing?

Did somebody say trivia? What about ants? Did you know there are 12,000 ant species worldwide? Which ant has the most painful sting in the world? The bullet ant. Ants are the longest living insects. How about shoes? Did you know men were the first to wear high heels? The most expensive shoes ever sold were the ruby red slippers from The Wizard of Oz. They sold for $660,000. Jimmy Choo created his first shoe at age eleven. Shall I keep going?

We looked at each other, then as if our heads were all attached by a single string, we swiveled to stare at the frog pressed against his terrarium, black eyes bulging. Slimy's throat throbbed in perfect rhythm to our shocked blinking.

Then, ever so slowly, every frown in the room turned upside down.

My grin was probably wider than it should have been, but we'd needed for something to go right. "We have our trivia expert. Lookout magician. Here comes Da Frog."

"Ribbit!" said Da Frog.

"Okay, what's next?" Sebille asked

Archie shuddered. "Then there's Dave. He's the last level of protection and...I'll be honest...I don't see you getting past him."

"Why not?" Sebille asked. "What could a guy named Dave possibly come at us with that we can't counter?"

"Dave isn't even a person. He's more a construct, magical AI. He specializes in mood and environmental magic."

"That doesn't sound so bad," Lea said.

"It's worse than you think," Archie disagreed. "His magic taps into your emotions and creates situations that confuse, terrorize, and imprison. Ugly stuff."

The dividing door slammed open and Hobs flew into the room, his big blue eyes wide and the light-brown tuft of hair on top of his head blown back with the force of his entrance.

"Miss!"

I turned to him. "What's wrong." Jumping to my feet, I let panic slide through me. "Is somebody hurt? Mr. Wicked? Baca?" I started toward the hobgoblin, looking him over for signs of injury. "Are you okay?"

Hobs swallowed hard, his small body all jittery. "That bad man's here. He's got Baca."

We found Jacob just inside the open garage-sized back door, leading to the dirt lot where the remains of Lea's once-beautiful greenhouse lay. Hobs and Baca must have been playing outside, and left the door open. I'd have to talk to them about that.

If we all survived the next few minutes.

The witch's darkly handsome face was hard, his blue eyes, so like Rustin's, glittered with rage. He settled his gaze on me as we approached. "How dare you send my sister after me. Did I not make myself clear on the situation for the fairies?"

Sebille strode over, looking surprisingly calm, though her iridescent green gaze promised pain for the evil witch. "We didn't send her. She insisted. We've been making plans to do as you asked. As you can imagine, it's no small undertaking."

He narrowed his gaze on her. "Don't try to play games with me, sprite, or you'll never see your mother again."

Her small intake of air was barely audible. "We wouldn't think of playing games," Sebille told him. "You have the upper hand. I won't do anything to harm my people. You will get your rune key. But the planning takes time."

He stared at her for a moment, then slid his gaze to me. "Don't think the sprite is the only one who will lose if you fail in this." He tightened the arm he held around Baca's throat and she began to struggle, her small face reddening as she fought to breathe.

"No!" My terrified gaze was locked on Baca. I wouldn't let the witch hurt her. Even if it meant he took me instead.

With a growl, Grym popped into his gargoyle form. "Let her be, Quilleran!"

"Uncle!" Rustin growled. He rushed past me, his fists clenched at his sides. Magic pulsed away from him, his chimera fighting to appear. A low growl, not even close to human, throbbed in his chest. "Stop right now or I'll make sure you pay."

I placed a hand on his arm. "Stand down, Rustin. You'll hurt Baca."

His muscles rock hard beneath my hand, my friend fought his need to shift and take on the man who'd caused him so much pain over the last couple of years.

Archie stepped up on the other side of me, no doubt hoping to distract Jacob from his nephew. "Quilleran, you wanker, what are you on about with this key? You know the Council will stop you using it. What's the point?"

Jacob laughed. If he had a superpower aside from his magic it would be his arrogance. In his mind, he was bullet-proof. Despite the fact that we'd bested him once before.

"Nobody will be able to stop me once I have the rune key," he told Archie dismissively. "I'll kill anyone who tries." He sneered at me. "I'll be able to take the Council myself if I want. You should find that more interesting than most, Naida keeper."

I glanced at my uncle, wanting to ask him what Jacob was talking about. He gave his head a little shake. He had no idea.

A white blur shot past me, hitting the witch in the chest and knocking him back a few inches. Jacob's grip on Baca's throat loosened. Jacob recovered quickly, grabbing Hobs and shaking him hard before flinging him away. Hobs smacked into the artifact shelves hard enough to rattle the magical objects, and slid bonelessly to the ground.

Sebille ran to his side.

Before Jacob could react, a feral snarl, followed by an enraged hiss sounded behind me, and green and gray streaks shot past, heading for the witch. Jacob took one look at the demon dog and Mr. Wicked, teeth and claws exposed, and took a step back. He flung a charcoal-gray haze of magic out to stop them from reaching him.

Vel lunged at the barrier, snarling. Wicked paced, looking for an opening in the magic.

"You have two days," the witch said. "Then, I'll extinguish the fairies."

Jacob grabbed Baca's arm and threw her high into the air, disappearing as she screeched in fear. Thank the goddess, Grym managed to catch her before she slammed into the concrete floor. He set her feet gently on the floor and ran out the door after Jacob. Rustin sprinted out too.

I hurried over to Baca. "Are you alright?" I asked the tiny brownie.

Baca nodded, tears glistening on her cheeks.

Hobs ran over and took her hand, stroking her back as she cried. He looked at me, his pale blue gaze hard with anger. "Miss, I'm going with you to Nom."

I started to shake my head.

Hobs straightened to his full height of twenty-six-ish inches. He pursed his full pink lips together and his eyes flashed. The light-brown tuft of hair between his oversized ears quivered with indignation. "I'm going, Miss. The bad man hurt our friends. I'm going to help you stop him."

I opened my mouth to argue, but Sebille put a hand on

my arm. "Let him come," she whispered, her expression unnaturally soft. "He wants to help."

I closed my mouth and sighed. "Okay. You can come."

"I'll keep an eye on Croakies," Baca said in her customarily soft voice. "You don't have to worry about things here while you're gone."

I gave her a smile. "Thank you, Baca. I really appreciate it."

Archie placed a hand on my shoulder. "May I speak to you privately for a moment, please?"

"Sure. Upstairs?"

He agreed and we climbed the steps to my apartment. I closed the door and headed into the kitchen. "Tea?"

He grimaced. Right. Making tea wasn't my strongest thing. In fact, I didn't make tea so much as lukewarm swamp water with floating chunks of bark. "Water?"

He shook his head. "This won't take long. I only wanted to let you know I spoke to your mother."

My pulse picked up as it always did when I thought about my mom. I'd thought she was dead for most of my life and had only been reacquainted with her and the brother I hadn't known I had a few months earlier. "Okay."

He seemed unwilling to hold my gaze. An icy sweat broke out on my forehead as I realized he wasn't going to give me good news. "She won't help."

Archie shook his head. "Not because she doesn't want to. It's just..." He finally looked into my eyes. "Narina's in the middle of a bit of a crisis and needs to stay where she is."

I tried not to be hurt. I really did. But the feeling of being abandoned again by my only living parent sprang too easily to life. After all, it was pretty much the default my family seemed to work under. "Got it. I suppose Eddie's with her?" Unlike me, my brother was always alongside my mother. It seemed she valued his talents as a chaos sorcerer over mine as a KoA.

"No, actually, he wants to help. He'll meet us there."

I felt my brows lift. "On Nom? How?"

Archie shrugged. "Narina and Eddie run in a different circle. I've given up questioning how they do anything."

"Can they tell us what we'll find in the vault?"

"No. I did ask them that, of course. But they don't have the knowledge to give us."

I narrowed my eyes. "That's a very careful way of putting it."

He shrugged. "Their words, I'm afraid." He shoved his hands into his pockets. "Well then. Off I go. I have work to do in finding those fairies." He stopped with his hand on the door handle. "Will you leave tomorrow?"

"It will depend on those moon calculations."

"Ah. Yes. Sleep well then, Naida."

"You too."

I stared at the door for a minute after he left, my emotions roiling. Fear, frustration, uncertainty, depression and loneliness were all churning in my mind, making me just want to lay down and take a nap. But there was no time for that. I had work to do to prepare for our trip.

So, with a long pull of air and a slow release, I forced my feet to move. Two days. Jacob Quilleran hadn't given us much time to pull off the universe's biggest heist.

12

I'M TOO SEXY FOR MY TUNIC...TOO SEXY FOR MY TUNIC...

A door slammed, and I jerked awake. Groaning, I lifted my head to squint at Sebille. She was carrying a large white box that smelled like heaven, her fire-engine red hair already plaited into a single long braid.

The sprite was wearing pants with many pockets, like cargo pants, but instead of being the usual khaki or camouflage fabric, the sprite's pants were purple and green plaid. To make things worse, she wore them with red sneakers and a violet, long-sleeved shirt.

So much for keeping a low profile. Between Sebille's hair and her outfit, she looked like a solar flare.

I wiped drool off my face, surreptitiously swiping my sleeve over the telltale wet spot on the table, and sat up, yawning. "What time is it?"

"Five o'clock."

My eyes popped wide. "In the evening?" Had I slept through a whole night and day?

She rolled her eyes so hard she could probably have

seen her brain. "Five in the morning. I found you snoring like a troll when I came in to make tea."

"Tea!" I said, rising like a brain-seeking zombie missile.

She placed the box onto the table, lifting a hand to stop me. "I'll get it. If you even so much as touch the pot, the tea comes out tasting like stagnant pond water with extra seaweed."

She wasn't wrong. Besides, that left me with first choice of the donuts.

"Meow," my cat announced as he entered the room. I turned to find the dividing door closing quietly behind him and shook my head. No closed door or window ever stopped Mr. Wicked. He seemed able to open any barrier in his path. If only he could open the locked doors of the vault in Nom, we'd be sitting pretty.

I was happily munching my second chocolate-covered glazed when Grym and Rustin showed up, both carrying oversized dark green back packs. I gave them a look. "Did you two coordinate outfits?"

"We just ran into each other outside," Grym said, looking slightly appalled.

"I offered to help him carry supplies," Rustin said.

The dividing door slammed open and a blur of white spun through the room. It halted only long enough to grab two chocolate cake donuts and spin back out of the room.

"You'd better grab donuts before Hobs comes back. He and Baca might look small, but they can fit a lot of donuts into those tiny frames."

Sure enough, I'd barely stopped talking before the hobgoblin was back. I tapped into my keeper magic to give me speed and grabbed his skinny wrist before he could get away. I wasn't fast enough to stop him from grabbing donuts, unfortunately. He already had two more chocolate covered glazed clutched in his long fingers. "That's all," I told him. "Leave some for everybody else."

He gave me a sheepish smile. "Yes, Miss."

As long as I'd captured the little guy, I gave him the once-over. He was wearing his customary white tunic and pants, but he'd added a tiny camo vest with pockets that were already bulging with something. "What have you got in those pockets?" I asked, not sure I wanted to know.

"Brownies."

Nope, shouldn't have asked. "Do you have any real food in there?"

Brownies are real food to hobgoblins, Mr. Slimy informed me.

I glanced over at the bug-eyed know-it-all. "Is that so?"

It is. They need the fat calories and their bodies transform the sugar into nutrients. Chocolate is particularly nutritious for them. Did you know a hobgoblin burns up twice as many calories pound-for-pound as a hummingbird?

I sighed. We'd created a trivia nightmare in the frog. "I didn't. But watching this one eat, I'm not surprised."

"He's right, Miss. I eat about ten thousand calories a day and still keep my girlish figure."

I eyed his skinny arms and legs, big head and curveless torso and snorted. "I can't tell you how jealous I am of that."

He reached under the arm I was holding and grabbed two more donuts. "Maybe if you ate more brownies and donuts, you could be too sexy for your tunic like me." Then he spun away, leaving a badly-sung chorus of "I'm Too Sexy" behind on the air.

I groaned, knocking my forehead against my hands. "Life's not fair."

The air at my back warmed and a strong arm wrapped

around me, pulling me close for a kiss on the temple. "You're perfect just the way you are. Have another donut."

I smiled up at Grym. "See, that's why I keep you around."

"Well," Sebille said, handing the guys each a cup of tea. "That and the fact that you bring us carryout food all the time."

I reached up and bumped knuckles with the sprite.

The front door jangled cheerfully as it opened. We all looked up to see Archie entering. He looked excited. "We figured out the moon phases. The triple moons are aligning now."

My eyes popped wide. "Now? Like right now?"

He glanced at his watch. "In about fifteen minutes."

I jumped up, looking right and left and unsure what to do first. "Oh my goddess! We need to go now!" In the next moment I started to panic. "I'm not ready."

Grym grabbed my shoulders and looked me in the eyes. "You put your backpack together?"

I nodded mutely.

"Go get it, grab the book, and we'll be waiting to leave as soon as you get back down here."

I nodded again, my mind spinning. "Right. I need to get my pack." I started toward the dividing door, stopped, and turned back. "Think I can stuff that box of donuts into my pack?"

Sebille came out of the tea area with a zippered plastic bag. "I'm way ahead of you. I have room in my bag."

Thank the goddess. We were going to Nom to invade the Universal Council's vault. We were going to go up against powerful guards, magical locks and wards, and too many blank spots in our knowledge.

There was a good chance I'd need a donut.

It would be a miracle if we succeeded. But, if we didn't succeed, the fairies would die. And we might die. Or we might spend the rest of our lives in jail.

My bowels twisted with alarm as I headed upstairs. I took several deep breaths and slowly released them. I needed to stay calm.

We could do this. I was surrounded by smart, powerful people and they all wanted to help.

It would be okay.

I mean, we'd survived the wraiths, right? We could survive a three-headed cat, a magician, and a guy named Dave.

It was all going to be okay.

Something crashed to the ground in the artifact library and I jumped, yelping. My nerves were seriously in a knot.

"Again!"

It was highly possible I was going to hurt the hobgoblin. "Hobs!" I yelled down, my tone none too happy. "We're leaving. Get your bag."

"Yes, Miss."

I SLAMMED down on the grass and stumbled forward trying to stay upright. The Book of Pages hit the ground next to me and shrank to its traveling size. I grabbed it, shoving it into my pocket as my team appeared around me with several soft pops of displaced air.

"Yowl!" Wicked objected, twisting around in my arms until I let him go. He jumped to the grass and stalked away, tail angrily snapping the air.

Hobs slammed into the ground in a tangle of spidery legs and arms and rolled, smacking up against a large tree with a grunt. He shot upright immediately and opened his mouth.

I stuck my finger in his face, "Don't!" My whisper was soft and urgent. "Keep the noise down."

"*Again...*" he whispered happily.

Are we there yet? Slimy asked from inside Sebille's pocket. She rolled her eyes. "You've asked me that five times already," she told him impatiently. "Yes. We're here."

I knew it, sayeth the all-knowing frog. *Do you know how many kinds of insects exist in the world?*

"No trivia yet, frog," Rustin growled. "We're not in the vault yet."

"How many?" Hobs asked with a grin, ever the straight man.

Ten quintillion, Slimy responded smugly.

"You made that up," I said. "Quintillion isn't even a real word."

Is too, Slimy insisted.

I looked at Lea and she shrugged. "I think he's right. It's a word."

It's trivia, baby.

I shared an alarmed glance with the sprite. It was possible the whole Trivia King thing was going to the frog's head. "Don't ever call me that again," I told him.

Whatever.

I looked around our group, taking inventory. Vel was a few feet away, sniffing around a tree. Hobs was there... Wicked, Slimy, Lea, Sebille, and Rustin. I saw everyone but my boyfriend. "Where's Grym?"

Panic barely had time to set in before Grym came striding around a large bush, his handsome face tight with worry. "I don't see the vault."

"Fish farts!" I mumbled. "Of course, it couldn't be that easy."

"Wait," Rustin said. "It has to be here. This looks exactly like the picture in Osvald's book."

We looked around the space, which consisted of a large flat area of grass surrounded by a bunch of trees and bushes. It all looked very normal and unassuming, except for the large, cone-shaped hill a dozen yards away across the grass. A single sapling tree stood at the very top of the hill, as if someone had planted it like a flag to show they'd been there. No great accomplishment. I was pretty sure that even with my rubbery, underutilized legs I could climb that hill.

In the distance, squatting under a thick layer of pale gray fog, was the castle I remembered seeing in Lea's book. "Maybe it's in the castle."

The group stared off into the distance at the palace, not commenting.

Movement out of the corner of my eye drew my attention to the little tree on top of the conical hill. It shimmied, briefly blurring before returning to normal. The change happened so fast I almost thought I'd imagined it. "Does that tree look right to you?" I asked the group. Vel suddenly appeared beneath the tree, having apparently climbed the hill from the other side. She was panting and her tail beat the air with excitement. "Vel, come down here," I called, whistling for extra incentive.

She promptly squatted next to the sapling, anointing it with her golden offering, then turned and disappeared from sight again.

Everybody stared at the tree for a beat and then dismissed it as unimportant.

A stick broke in the brush behind us and we spun around to face whatever was coming. Tension thrummed through the group as we waited, listening for the sounds of approaching trouble. Just when I was starting to think the noise had been nothing, a tall form emerged from the trees and sauntered toward us.

Vel came around the hill barking, her black eyes shiny with warning.

The newcomer spared the demon dog only a quick glance and then looked at me.

A little over six feet tall, the man had curly blond hair and dark blue eyes like the ones I saw in the mirror every day. Still too lean in my opinion, he looked healthier, with better color than he'd had when I'd seen him last. Eddie was no longer too pale, and his broad shoulders were squared, his steps full of vigor.

Hobs gave a little squeal and ran toward my brother, Wicked hot on his heels.

Eddie caught Hobs with a laugh and ruffled the tuft of hair on his head. "Young Hobs. How are you?" He tugged gently on the camo vest. "I like the addition. Very GI Joe."

Hobs preened. "It has pockets!" the hobgoblin exclaimed. "I filled them with brownies."

"Of course you did," Eddie laughed. Like the hobgoblin, my brother favored skinny pants and tunics with wide belts, his outfit reminiscent of the knights of the round table. Whether it was their sense of style, or something else, the two of them seemed to have a special affinity for each other.

Eddie bent down to run a hand along Wicked's back. "Mr. Wicked. Do you have things well in hand?" He held his knuckles out to Vel who sniffed them first and then gave them an enthusiastic lick.

My cat meowed plaintively, as if we were more trouble than we were worth.

Eddie straightened, giving Lea a shy smile. "Lea. How are you?"

She actually blushed. "I'm fine. It's good to see you again."

I smiled at my older brother, the months of being apart disappearing as he smiled back at me. "Hey, Eddie," I said.

He surprised me by grabbing me around the waist and lifting me off the ground in a hug.

I giggled like a school girl, then wrapped my arms around him and inhaled his familiar scent. "It's been too long."

He ruffled my hair as if I were ten instead of quickly gaining on thirty. "It has. You're looking good. You have a sparkle in your eyes and roses in your cheeks."

I flushed with pleasure. "That's a touch of madness you're seeing."

Eddie laughed.

Grym joined us, offering Eddie a hand and wrapping an arm around my waist. "Chaos Sorcerer Griffith."

Eddie's smile turned knowing. "Detective Grym. I see why Naida looks so happy."

It seemed an odd thing to point out under the circumstances, but I realized with a start that I was...happy. Not about our current mess, of course. But just generally.

"Hey," Sebille said, offering my brother a skinny, freckled hand.

"None of that, now." His smile softened and he took her hand, pulling her in for a hug. "We're going to fix this," he told the sprite.

To my surprise, she nodded, sniffling as tears glistened in her startling gaze. "Thank you for helping us."

"Of course." He stepped back and looked around, nodding at Rustin. "No Archie?"

"He stayed back to search for the fairies," Grym said, frowning. "Hopefully, he'll find them before we have to steal the key."

I understood Grym's pain. Being a cop made his part in our illegal mission awkward. But his protective side wouldn't let us go without helping. It was a pickle for sure. From his perspective, they were two poor choices. But I was glad he'd picked the poor choice that kept him with us.

"Understood. Well, shall we find this vault and get to it?" Eddie asked. The group started off across the grass. Eddie grabbed my arm, holding me back. "Mom wanted me to tell you she's really unhappy about not being able to come." His frown told me he was just as unhappy.

"Why couldn't she?" There was a note of anger in my tone. I regretted it. But it was hard not to feel that way. It seemed Narina Griffith always had something better to do than be with her daughter.

"She couldn't get away. Actually, she's doing what she needs to be doing right now, Naida. Please trust me on that."

I sighed. "Okay. I'll trust you. But I won't lie. I'm disappointed."

He gave me a quick, one-armed hug. "Understood."

"Meow!!! Hsss!" Wicked spit and yowled angrily from somewhere near the base of the hill. I didn't see him at first, given that the area was thick with bushes. A moment later, the bushes rustled and he stepped out, tail snapping angrily.

He was carrying something in his mouth. At first, I thought it was a squirrel or a rat and I opened my mouth to yell at him to let it go. But Wicked wobbled slightly in his step, dropping to the ground and rolling over what I realized was a stuffed toy. The toy was big enough for a dog, but had clearly been made for a cat.

I quickly realized it had been infused with something

special. Wicked flailed his paws at the toy, missing it and clawing the air. His orange eyes looked unfocused and he was making a purr/snarl/purr noise I'd never heard before. The movements were wild and...inebriated.

"Judging by the way your cat is acting, I'd say that thing has catnip in it," Rustin said, shoving his wire-rimmed glasses up his nose.

"There's only one reason there'd be a catnip toy at the bottom of this hill," I said, eyeing the little tree at the top.

"There's a large, three-headed cat nearby," Grym agreed. "But where?"

The little tree shimmered again, blurred, and then settled. A soft breeze blew past, smelling of flowers and freshly cut grass. But there were no flowers around. And there was definitely nobody mowing the grass. "Something's weird," I murmured.

"What was that?" Rustin asked.

I glanced in the direction he was looking. I saw nothing. "What?"

He pointed a little bit wildly.

"Did you sniff Wicked's catnip?" Grym teased.

Sebille and I laughed, thinking of Rustin's giant kitty slash dragon form snorting catnip.

He glared at us. "There was an opening there." He frowned. "I think."

"This is a glamour," Eddie said with a surety that told me he'd seen it before. "I'll bet the vault is covered by a three-dimensional glamour."

Sebille lifted her hands and threw magic at it.

A few spots in the grass exploded upward, but nothing else happened.

"I don't think it's a glamour," Sebille said.

"It is," Eddie assured her. He walked from one end to the other, kicking at the bushes and peering closely at the hill.

"How do we get rid of it?" I asked, because, yeah, I could always be counted on for a stupid question or two.

Eddie glanced my way. "You should all step back."

We did as he requested, though I had no idea what he could do to remove a glamour if Sebille hadn't been successful.

Eddie lifted his hands above his head and went very still. His blue gaze fractured. Random shapes and colors flared and roiled, shifting within his eyes like shattered glass, and filtering a kaleidoscope of light in a thousand different directions.

A thin sheen of multi-hued energy slipped over him, snugging itself to his skin like a micro-thin wetsuit. Chaotic waves of power roiled and spun away from him like starbursts. The power shifted space and then sucked it back, only to turn it upside down with a soft moan of air bumping up against unnatural energy. Gradually, each wave of power gathered up a chunk of the hill and tugged it away, the newly collected space floating in random whirls above the ground. A triangle of grass swirled around a square of bush, bumping against a star-shaped hunk of tree. The energy waves came faster, slamming into the hillside and cutting away dirt-colored fractals that spiraled faster and faster, striking against each other as they sped like ions being heated in a beaker on top of an open flame.

Pressure built in front of us. The ground beneath our feet quaked. And the general feeling in the area was one of expectancy, like the air just before lightning slams into a building, supercharging the electrical input inside.

A strong wind had risen, blowing debris around us and whipping my hair into my face in painful slaps.

Vel woofed, the sound filled with fear. She threw back her head and howled.

That wasn't good. That was really not good. "Take cover!" I screamed to everyone else. My voice was like smelling salts, tearing them from their stupors, and we all turned away and started to run.

We'd barely reached the copse of trees where we'd entered Nom, before the small hill in front of us detonated in an explosion of heat, light and color that obliterated everything else around it.

13

IS THAT A HAIRBALL?

All that was left behind was reality. Or, what passed for reality on Nom.

Where there had once been a faux hill and a fake sapling, had become an arched entrance with a heavy metal door. It reminded me of the entrance to a bunker. Lights blinked across its stainless-steel surface, flashing a code in red, green, and yellow illumination that I couldn't decipher.

As the literal dust cleared, my eyes sought out my brother. What I found had me pushing to my feet and running. "Eddie!"

He was lying on his back in front of the oversized door, his face covered in soot and dirt and his clothing torn and filthy. His eyes were open, staring up into a cloudless blue sky, and for a terrifying moment, I thought he was gone.

I dropped to my knees and touched his arm. "Eddie, talk to me."

He blinked slowly, like a turtle, and groaned. "Well, that got away from me faster than expected."

I barked out a relieved laugh. "Not necessarily. I've seen your handiwork before. That seemed just about right."

Vel trotted over and kissed Eddie's ear, making him jolt in surprise. The little dog dropped to her haunches, panting, and gave him soft eyes.

"Um," he said, eyeing her with uncertainty. "You haven't introduced me to your new friend."

"That's Vel. She's a demon dog. She likes to stir things up. Literally. She messes with time, physical location, movement. You were just speaking her language."

Eddie pushed to a seat and smiled at the little dog. "Where did you get her?"

"The demonic realm," Grym answered for me. With a grin, he offered my brother a hand up. "That was really something else," he said.

Eddie bowed his head. "Thank you?" He chuckled. "My control needs a little work. You'd think I'd have a better handle on it by now. I've been working on it for most of my life."

"Chaos magic is tough," Rustin said, joining us. "It's..."

"Chaotic?" Eddie offered. The three men chuckled as if it had been the best joke in the world.

"Maybe we could get back to this?" Sebille said, her tone brimming with impatience. She was standing in front of the metal door, her palms flat on its surface as if she were reading it. The frog was no longer in her pocket. He was sitting fat and flabby on her shoulder, his black eyes bulging blankly.

The magic doesn't feel like anything I've ever encountered, Slimy said. *Maybe the chaos sorcerer can just blow it up.*

Eddie shook his head. "We need to keep damage to a minimum," he warned, sliding his gaze over the group. "Blowing up a glamour is one thing. But doing irreparable damage to the structure or the guardians is pretty much an assurance of prison."

Sebille's voice pulled our attention back to the job at hand. "I actually think this is an archaic form of fae magic."

Lea joined her, placing her palms over the surface. Soft green light sifted from her palms and her expression turned contemplative. "I think you're right." She stepped away. "Can you open it?"

Sebille sighed. "I'm a bit rusty on the old stuff, but I'll give it a try."

To my surprise, she popped into her sprite form, buzzing slowly over the door from top to bottom. As her magic bathed the metal, the surface darkened and appeared to soften beneath her hands. She swirled her hands in overlapping circles as she flew over the door. Her wings made a strange whirring sound I'd never heard before as she worked.

After several minutes, the lights flashing across the surface of the door changed their pattern, briefly sped, and then slowed. One by one, they blinked out.

The big door slid soundlessly open, culminating in a loud click as it disappeared into the wall.

We stood silent, staring into the large empty space within the door.

"Does anybody else think that was too easy?" Grym asked. His deep voice seemed more rumbly than usual, as if he were a heartbeat away from shifting into his gargoyle.

A taut silence stretched between us, a sense of unhappy expectation painting the air. The interior of the vault was comprised of some kind of green-tinted metal I didn't recognize, its walls the same arched shape as the exterior door. The floor looked like rubber. I couldn't see the ceiling from where we stood. It reached pretty high and was lost in shadows.

A white and camo blur shot past us, with Wicked and Vel hot on Hobs' heels.

I started moving, knowing from experience that trouble was more likely than not to find the trio.

The rest of the group followed us inside. Vel and Wicked sniffed the floor, Wicked checking any nooks for dust motes he could torture. Reassured they weren't going to leap immediately into trouble, I glanced around. "No sign of the Nomook, I said."

"I wouldn't be too sure of that," Grym said. He was crouching near one wall, Vel snuffling around his feet. He lifted something off the floor and carried it over.

"Is that a hairball?" Sebille asked with a grimace.

"Just a fur tumbleweed." He eyed it carefully. "Looks like our Nomook is an orange tiger cat."

"Fun!" Lea said. "I've always wanted a tiger cat."

"Maybe this one will let you adopt it," Rustin teased.

"Maybe it will," Lea said, grinning at him.

"Well, apparently this thing stinks at guarding the front door," I said with a shake of my head. "We might as well keep moving. If we're lucky all the guardians have gone to a team-building event offsite and we'll have a free road ahead."

Sebille snorted.

Hobs and Vel were already halfway across the wide space, heading toward a door in the center of the end wall. I frowned at that door. "Weird question. How's a cat supposed to open a door?"

"Wicked does it all the time," Sebille said.

"True. But he's special," I said smugly.

"He has magic," Grym corrected. "I'm sure the Nomook does too."

"Where's the litterbox," Lea asked.

I pointed to a couple of terrifyingly large bowls along the wall, and a carpeted structure wider than my car and nearly as tall as the room. I assumed it was a scratching post. "Maybe over by that other stuff."

Rustin wrinkled his nose. "It smells like cat in here. He's been here recently."

Wicked threw an insulted yowl over his shoulder and followed his friends toward the door I hoped led to the next section of the vault. His annoyance was clear in the way his tail whipped the air behind him. My cat walked right up to the door and smacked into it with his face, bouncing off with an indignant yowl.

"Wicked tried to use his door mojo and it didn't work," Sebille said, grinning. "Dumb cat."

As if he understood her, Wicked whipped around and hissed at the sprite.

She laughed.

"I'll get it," Hobs declared. He wrapped his spidery fingers around the handle, tugging. A beat later, his big feet were pressed against the door and he was hanging from the knob, hammering on it with everything he had.

The door is magic, you derf, Slimy said.

Wicked hissed again.

"Shut it, frog," I told slimy. "You're upsetting Mr. Wicked."

Seems to me the cat is too sensitive.

"Your *friend*," I said, emphasizing the word. "Is out of his element. Have a little compassion. We're all feeling stressed."

"Maybe we can revisit the therapy session *after* we get the key and get out of here?" Sebille snarked.

I glared at her.

"Hsssss....rrrrrrrar!"

"Now what's his problem?" Grym asked. "He's certainly jumpy today."

Vel ran up to Wicked and dropped to her haunches beside him, lifting her gaze to a spot high above our heads. She barked, the fur on her shoulders lifting.

Being mere human-ish and therefore much slower on the uptake than the animals, we all scanned our gazes upward. To the ceiling.

"Crusty cat cooties," I murmured in horror. "We're all gonna die."

The cat...Nomook...was as big as an elephant. Each of its three heads the size of a brown bear, with teeth that would make that bear proud.

I knew about the teeth because the three-headed feline was currently cleaning the enormous things, using claws that were as long as my hands.

The Nomook's three heads were perfectly still on its big body, its slanted green eyes locked on us without a hint of concern. But its tails...yep, there were three of them... swayed with just a little too much umph for a truly laid-back feline.

The guardian was draped across a heavy metal support beam high above us. It was one of several of the things that were clearly not there for structural support.

"It's a giant jungle gym for monsters," Grym said, a soft growl in his voice. "Now, I've seen everything."

"That's a big beast," Rustin said. "Should I break out the chimera?"

"Let's keep that on the back burner," I told him. "Like

Eddie said, we don't want to hurt the guardians if we can avoid it."

"How do you propose we fight it then?" Grym ground out.

"Very carefully," Eddie said, the hint of a smile curving his lips.

Yep. There was the Griffith sense of humor. Warped as it was. I knew I'd gotten it from somewhere.

"Do you think it's just going to sit up there and watch us?" Lea asked.

"Miss?" Hobs tugged on my sleeve, but I couldn't drag my gaze from the Nomook. "Not right now, Hobs."

I really wished I knew more about the creature staring down at us. I'd tried to do research on it before we left but had found nothing. What I wouldn't give to have Archie there with us. He was an endless font of scientific information.

A thought occurred. "Trivia King? What do you know about this thing?"

I could almost feel Slimy puckering from inside Sebille's pocket. *Nothing. I've never heard of it before.*

"It's anti-mythological," Eddie said. "The Nomook doesn't exist in mythology. In fact, it doesn't exist anywhere else in the universe. It's a magical construct created by one of the Council members, strictly to serve as a Nom guardian."

"Why a cat?" Sebille asked, grimacing. The sprite was not really a cat person. She basically just put up with Wicked because I made her. Plus, he was smart and magically gifted, so he came in handy more than I did. Actually, almost everybody came in handy...magically speaking... more than I did.

Eddie shrugged. "I guess she likes cats."

I stared into the pretty slanted eyes of the thing...all six of them...and couldn't help thinking how cute it must have been as a kitten. Had it been a kitten? Surely the Council hadn't magically conjured the thing as an adult. That would have been a seriously missed opportunity.

"Um, Miss?" Hobs tugged on my sleeve again.

I jerked around, annoyed. "What is it, Hobs?"

He pointed down at the floor. It took me a beat to see what he was trying to show me. Some kind of string was puddled on the floor around our feet. No, that wasn't quite right. Thick and fuzzy, it looked more like...

"Yarn?" Lea said, frowning.

It was the size of a strong rope, but looked like yarn. I had no doubt it was much stronger than yarn, though.

"Cats love to play with yarn," Hobs said.

Wicked yowled, flying off the ground and spinning in midair. He was biting at something wrapped around his middle and by the time I figured it out, my feet had been yanked together and I was flying, upside down, toward the ceiling and the monster waiting on the cross beam for me to arrive. My scream was cut short as the air in my lungs whooshed out from sheer terror.

One by one, my team yelped in alarm, the sound of string sliding over metal filled the air. My yarn stopped moving and I tried to look around at my friends, but found that the movement sent me spinning in a dizzying twirl.

Wooziness swamped me and I instinctively reached out to still the movement. But there was nothing to grab. And things were about to get worse.

I suddenly found myself staring into three massive furry faces with terrifyingly big teeth.

"Nice...um...kitty-kitty."

I needn't have worried about the teeth though. It was the

claws that came at me first. Or at least the paws, which looked to be the size of my entire body. Unfortunately, while the Nomook was fashioned to appear as a cat, it clearly didn't believe in retracting its claws.

I shrieked and tried to curl into a fetal position to protect my mushy middle from the blow coming my way. I was only partially successful. A black, rock-hard pad hit me on the hip and pain sheared through me. I barely noticed the pain. The blow sent me swinging violently. Nausea rose up and I had to close my eyes to keep from losing all those donuts I shouldn't have eaten.

But closed eyes didn't save my stomach from lurching with every swing of the yarn.

I had to do something and fast, or I was going to embarrass myself in a big way.

A sharp scream made my eyes snap open. Lea was being batted around, but not as hard as the Nomook had batted me. That was the good news. The bad news was that it was batting her back and forth between two paws, which doubled the body blows and kept her way too close to the thing's teeth.

"Somebody do something," I yelled. "It's going to kill her."

"Coming, Miss!" Hobs called.

That was when I realized my mistake. "No, Hobs. Not you. Stay back!"

Too late, a white and camo blur flew through the air, landed on top of the middle head, and shot away again before one of the paws could grab him.

He'd left a furry stuffed mouse behind.

Goddess, no. Not the catnip!

14

TUCK AND ROLL, MISS!

The Nomook shook its head and the toy dropped to the floor.

Light flashed across the room. My gaze flew to Grym in his gargoyle form. He ripped the string of his swinging prison and leaped to the floor. "Here kitty, kitty. Come and get me."

The Nomook swung its heads toward Grym, three tails whipping the air behind it.

Sebille assumed her sprite form in another flash of light. She buzzed away from the restraints, heading for Lea.

The Nomook's heads swung in her direction.

"Hey, stupid!" Grym shouted. He threw the catnip toy at the monster, pulling its attention away from Lea.

The Nomook snagged the toy on a curved claw and rubbed its left head against it. A deep rumble filled the over-sized room, throbbing against the walls and echoing in my teeth and bones.

The head holding the toy was wobbling, the eyes going crossed as it rubbed its face over the stuffed mouse.

Keeping one eye on the soon-to-be-intoxicated cat, I struggled to break the string holding me aloft.

Far below me, Vel started barking and snarling, her tiny green form bouncing off the floor with every bark. The Nomook's center head turned toward my dog, its eyes narrowing as it presumably tried to figure out what it was looking at.

To my horror, it decided the little dog was worth a second look, and leaped from the crossbeam, landing with more grace and lightness than seemed possible given its size.

I yelped, ducking as one of the cat's tails swished in my direction. I managed to avoid a direct hit, but the snapping tail hit my string and sent me flying. I soared over the heads and the intoxicated one engaged a paw, swiping lazily at me as I flew past.

A white and camo blur hit my string and my stomach lurched as Hobs' arrival sent me into new eruptions of movement. The world spun dizzyingly. The movement blew my hair away from my face, and then into it as I swung back the other way. My stomach roiled, threatening to reintroduce all of us to my slightly processed donuts. "Bleurgh," I moaned.

Hobs shrieked happily as I completed an arc and started back through another one.

"Hobs, cut her loose!" Grym yelled from below.

He was trying to stay beneath me in my wild pendulum swings, his arms outstretched to catch me when I fell. Without warning, he sank downward on a startled yell, disappearing into the rubbery floor.

"Grym!" I screamed.

A big hand appeared above the hole and he tried to claw his way out, but seemed to be having trouble.

Across the room, Vel was snarling and lunging at the cat. Fortunately, the little dog was on the creature's intoxicated side. The Nomook's enormous head was wobbling, its eyes crossing, and the paw was slashing at the air all around Vel, but missing her.

The head on the right was hissing at Grym, claws raised to slash at him as he finally pulled himself free of the floor.

Sebille was pinned to the ground by one of the cat monster's tails and Lea...

I couldn't find my friend. Or Rustin. I hoped that meant they were working on getting us through the door and out of the Nomook's clutches.

Grym took two steps and started sinking again. The floor appeared like quicksand beneath him and he was heavy in his gargoyle form, making him a perfect victim for the trick.

I yelled in frustration. Disaster rained down everywhere I looked.

"Hold on, Miss!" Hobs slashed something across the rope that was holding me aloft and it jerked. I dropped a few inches as he severed part of its width.

My terrified gaze shooting upward, I felt my eyes go wide. "Hobs, maybe there's a better way."

He grinned at me. "Tuck and roll, Miss!" Then he slashed a small blade across the remaining rope and I plunged downward on a hoarse scream.

I slammed into something leathery, pain radiating from my tailbone to my teeth, which I might have broken when they clacked together upon landing.

But I soon forgot the pain, as I looked up into a large, furry face, and heard the telltale rumble of a hunting cat when it's found its prey. The Nomook had me.

"Uh, guys!" I rasped out, my throat closing up with fear.

The cat licked its lips, its long whiskers twitching.

"We're working on it," Lea screamed.

"Use non-lethal methods only!" Eddie yelled.

I tore my gaze to my brother, who sounded very close by. To my shock, I found him climbing the intoxicated side of the Nomook.

"Have you lost your mind?" I hissed.

He grinned. "Just give me a minute and we'll be good." I watched in horror as he reached the monster's shoulder, then had to duck as the catnip toy swung his way. To my surprise, he leaped up and grabbed hold of the toy, smearing it with something black.

"Wait, is that...?"

The center head spotted Eddie and swung toward him with a hiss. He abandoned ship, leaping to the ground and rolling safely away. But as he climbed to his feet, the floor seemed to melt away beneath him, sinking him to his waist.

A moment later, a second catnip toy hit the ground next to him. Eddie reached into his pocket and came up with more duplicating artifact, quickly smearing it over the toy on the ground.

Without warning, the Nomook lifted onto its back paws and batted at something in the air. I squinted at a small cluster of dust motes. No. It was magic. Like a thousand tiny stars, the silvery mass grew steadily, sparkling like stars and just as enticing.

Sebille sent another wave of the stuff toward the monster and buzzed away before a flailing paw could knock her out of the air.

The center head had gone wobbly, a second catnip mouse clutched in its mouth. The eyes that swung my way looked unfocused.

Grym managed to get to the third catnip mouse Eddie had created with replicating dust. He flung it at the head on the right before sinking to his knees again. But he was getting faster at climbing out. He took off toward the Nomook as soon as he scrambled free, dodging around its massive legs and heading for me.

The Nomook yowled, then unceremoniously dropped me to snag the toy from the air. I landed against a firm chest and strong arms pulled me in.

"Let's go," Grym said in his rumbly gargoyle voice. He set me on my feet and grabbed my hand. We started to run.

The floor sank and rolled beneath my feet, until it was like running in deep sand. I stumbled several times and Grym sank to his ankles once before fighting his way out.

Behind us, the Nomook fell to the ground, rolling around with its toys, so intoxicated that two of its three tails got tangled together and its back feet couldn't figure out how to catch the ground.

The third tail snapped against the floor inches from the door Sebille and Rustin were trying to open. Slimy was on the floor in front of it, no doubt giving them magical advice and Lea was crafting a spell, Eddie standing guard as they all worked.

Something clicked overhead and water shot out of sensors in the ceiling. The water was icy cold and immediately yanked the cat monster out of its drugged fog. The creature dropped its toys and shot to its feet, no longer intoxicated.

So much for our little catnip trick. I glanced at Lea. "How's that spell coming along?" I yelled.

She held up two fingers. I didn't know if that was two seconds, minutes, hours, or days. Whichever it was, her spell would probably be too late.

Vel was still harassing the creature, dancing around its

big paws and nipping at its legs and paws whenever she got the chance.

I had a thought.

"Vel, time to slow things up."

The little dog stopped barking and dropped to her haunches, looking at me with her black tongue hanging out.

For a minute, I thought she hadn't understood. But then her little chest puffed up, her bright black eyes widened, and a low rumble started in her chest.

Panic slashed through me, tightening my chest. I might have requested her special kind of magic, but I was suddenly having second thoughts. Vel's magic was scary strong. And I suddenly remembered Eddie's non-lethal magic warning. I took a step toward my dog. "Vel...don't..."

"Take cover!" Grym bellowed.

Everybody scattered, ducking behind anything we could find. I grabbed Wicked, and Hobs snatched the frog off the floor.

"WOOF!"

There was a stark moment of expectant silence and then...

Whoosh...

I closed my eyes, cringing in expectation of what I knew was coming.

A sonic boom blasted through the room and shot out through the big door. The Nomook lifted into the air and then dropped back into place with a thud that shook the walls.

Sounding oddly distant to my bruised eardrums, Vel's barking grew shriller. Each bark ending with a snarl too big to belong to the tiny dog.

Magic brushed against my skin.

Familiar magic.

I opened my eyes and looked at the scene mere inches from my eyes. I blinked.

The Nomook blinked.

Vel blinked, her tail giving a tentative wag.

"Meow?" the big creature said.

Vel's tail stopped wagging. The magic hadn't worked. The beast must have been too big to contain.

"Hey," I said, giving the monster a small wave.

It started toward us, three fangy smiles promising death. The low rumble in its chest wasn't a purr.

"Does anybody have a Plan B?" Eddie asked from where he was crouching behind a really big water bowl.

"Plan B?" Then my scattered mind cleared. "Goddess in a girl-band. How did I forget my Ace in the hole?" I held up a finger and the Nomook started to growl. Quickly divesting myself of my back pack, I unzipped it. Keeping one eye firmly on the monster across from me. I dug around in the pack, fingers searching for Plan B.

The Nomook stood up and started toward me, all six eyes locked onto my movements. Grym popped up from behind a scratching post that was big enough for mountain climbers to scale. "Hey there, bet you can't get me."

The taunt distracted the monster long enough for my fingers to land on Plan B. "Aha!"

All six eyes flashed back my way. "Oops." I tugged the object out and held it in front of the Nomook. "See. Doesn't this look like fun?"

One of the heads cocked slightly, ears twitching.

I glanced at my favorite little hat feather. The artifact was a cheerful little thing that loved to dance. "Can you stay out of reach, but draw it out the door?" I asked softly, releasing the feather.

It gave me a playful little curtsy and shot away, safely over the Nomook's heads.

To my delight, the Nomook swung around and darted after the little feather, its thundering footsteps carrying it right out of the vault.

Every eye in the place turned my way. The air around me chilled under their hostile stares. My smile died a slow death. "What?"

"You didn't think to do that sooner?" Sebille snarled.

"Um...sorry?"

Snick!

"The door's open," Rustin announced, then slid me a glare. "No thanks to Naida."

Le cringe. "Aw, come on."

Shaking his head with disgust, Eddie handed the replication powder back to me. "You dropped this when you were hanging upside down." His tone was cool and he looked at me as if I'd really let him down.

"Come on, guys. I was a little distracted in there." I followed them through the door, jumping as it slammed shut behind me. The soft snick of a lock sliding into place made my throat go dry.

Shoving fear away, I looked around at our next challenge.

The second area was much darker than the first section had been. The high curved walls were lost behind some kind of curtain and the ceiling was obscured by darkness. Multi-hued motes of magic danced around our legs, their soft, fluttering illumination the only thing lighting the enormous space.

Music kicked in, filling the space, and someone yelped in surprise. I arched a brow at Grym and he shrugged. "It startled me."

I grinned.

The light show jumped into motion, the number of motes increasing even as the music sped. It was loud enough that I could barely hear myself think. There was no way we could carry on a conversation. The motes rose above our heads, their movements perfectly tuned to the thundering rock music. The combination of music and frantic movement was giving me a headache. I wanted to close my eyes but I recognized a magic preview when I saw one. Something was coming. What we were experiencing was simply the warmup act.

The music crescendoed with a brain-bleed-inducing drum riff and a twangy guitar solo and then died. All the pretty little lights snapped off, leaving us in darkness.

The silence was almost a physical presence. If it weren't for the ringing in my ears, I'd have enjoyed the quiet. Even knowing it had to be the calm before the storm.

Right on cue, two large spotlights clicked on, and we were looking at a raised stage with thick folds of red velvet draping behind it.

And in the very center stood an average-sized man with a large nose and small hands. He was wearing a tux with long tails, glossy black shoes, and a really tall black hat.

A large, glittering sign hung from the draperies behind him. The sign read, "Stump The Trivia King."

Hello, magician.

15

EXTRATERRESTRIALS, DUST, AND TIME-TRAVELING TORTOISES

*O*h, heck no! sayeth the frog. *He's not the trivia king. I am.*

"How about let's not antagonize the crazy man with the tall hat," I murmured.

Right on cue, the man doffed his tall hat and bowed in our direction. "Welcome. Welcome one and all. Wonders galore await as you learn the secrets of the universe nobody even knew were secrets. You'll learn what you never learned before and consume knowledge heretofore unconsumable. In short, you'll find your minds blown. Your brains bested. And your thoughts made thoughtful. Are you ready to begin?"

I held up a hand, "Er, hi. I'm Naida. What exactly do you have in mind?"

He frowned at me. "Why, trivia of course. What else? Can't you read the sign?"

Behind me, Sebille chuckled darkly.

I turned to glare at her, sliding my glower to include the bug-eyed bunion squatting on her shoulder. The frog was also laughing.

"Who will you name as your champion?" tall hat asked, his voice booming around the space.

I grimaced. "Uh, him?" I pointed at the frog.

It was Slimy's turn to glower as tall hat broke into hysterics.

"A frog? You're depending on a frog for your very lives?"

"Our very lives?" I scanned my group with a worried frown. "Did anybody know this was a trivia duel to the death?"

They shook their heads. All except for Eddie. He was frowning. He stepped forward. "Trivia King, I believe the standard language in the contract refers to play for passage. I don't remember seeing a death addendum."

Tall hat blew air through his lips and flapped a hand. "I'm the talent, son. I decide the terms. Take them or leave them."

We huddled.

"You want me to eat him?" Rustin asked.

"Tempting," Grym said. He glanced at my brother. "But I'm guessing that's a no go?"

Eddie shook his head. "Let me speak to him."

We watched Eddie stride toward the stage. Tall hat watched him too, a smug look on his face that made me want to choke him with his own trivia. There was a heated exchange which I couldn't, unfortunately, interpret from that distance. Eddie returned to us, his expression not giving me much hope.

"Well?" Sebille urged.

"He's sticking to his guns on the rule change. Unfortunately, *our* rules don't change. We can't hurt him."

"Then how are we going to win passage through here?" I asked.

"We'll need to win," Eddie said.

"Uh, guys..."

We turned to Lea.

"What're Hobs and the kids doing?" she asked.

I swung my glance toward the stage, where the three culprits were stalking the magician. "That can't be good," I murmured.

The smug magician at the front of the raised platform seemed oblivious to the threesome stalking his way. I opened my mouth to stop whatever was about to go down, but I was too late. Tall hat yanked a wand from his pocket and swung around, "Abra-ka-grabya!" Magic shot from the wand and he waved it from one side of the stage to the other, encompassing all three trouble seekers in a pale-yellow haze. A moment later, the haze solidified and they were behind glass.

Hobs pounded on the glass, his blue eyes wide. He was yelling at us but I couldn't hear a word. Wicked frowned at the enclosure, batting it with a paw before stalking along the walls looking peeved. Vel sat down and wagged her tail, her black eyes bright with interest.

At that moment, I was less worried about tall hat, and more concerned about what my small assistants might do. "You don't want to do that," I told him. "They don't like being cooped up."

Tall hat's smug grin widened. "Then your frog had better deliver, hadn't he?"

I sighed, shaking my head. "Let's just get this done. I'm getting pretty sick of this place."

Sebille stepped forward and placed Mr. Slimy on the floor in front of us. He stared toward the magician, throat working and eyes bulging.

Tall hat lifted his wand and a bell dinged. "Today's

topics: Extraterrestrials, Dust, and Time-Traveling Tortoises."

Hope swelled in my chest. Slimy should definitely have the Tortoise thing down. We'd gone all the way back to the Jurassic era on Tildy the time-traveling tortoise. I remembered he'd been a squishy green know-it-all about tortoises at the time.

"Let us begin," the magician yelled into the darkness. "First subject. Extraterrestrials. He jabbed the wand at Slimy. "First strike goes to the frog."

The name's Mr. Slimy, the frog responded snottily.

Tall hat rolled his eyes. "Whatever. Go."

"Sebille, you have a long, lost brother," I muttered.

"Har de har, Naida," the sprite responded crankily.

The movie Alien was originally titled, Star Beast. Slimy began.

Tall hat blinked. "I'm not sure..."

Scientists believe aliens might look just like us.

"You mean short, green, and squishy?" Sebille asked the frog, laughing.

The magician swung his wand and a loud "Eehhh!" sound filled the room. "No comments from the audience." He whipped a finger toward Slimy. "Researchers believe aliens are hibernating, awaiting a cooler era."

The only confirmed use of Area 51 is as a flight-testing facility.

"People who work in Area 51 have to fly in through a restricted terminal at McCarran Airport on an unmarked plane that's allowed to pass through the airspace above Area 51."

People's fascination with alien life started in the early 17th century, when Galileo's new telescope allowed them to see the heavens in more detail.

"In 1848 a science teacher Thomas Dick estimated that

the number of aliens living inside the Solar System was twenty-two trillion."

Scientists believe that aliens on water-dense moons would probably look like giant squids.

We all chuckled at that one.

The magician straightened up, his expression filled with glee and said, "Twelve moon maidens have lived on the Eastern edge of Nom for a thousand years." He jabbed the wand into the air and a chime sounded. The sign behind the stage lit up and his name flashed with multi-hued lights similar to the ones we'd seen when we'd entered.

The word WINNER flashed across the sign several times, interspersed with the magician's self-claimed title.

"The Trivia King wins the first round," he exclaimed proudly.

Outraged cries burst forth from the audience.

"That's not fair," Sebille yelled. "You can't pick yourself."

"Cheat!" Lea yelled, giving him an enthusiastic thumbs down.

Rustin growled and showed teeth that were decidedly larger than they should be.

Inside his glass prison, Hobs pounded angrily on the restraining wall and Wicked yowled in silent agreement.

Vel sat happily, tail sweeping the floor and eyes still bright.

A score board appeared at the side of the room, proclaiming: Trivia King – one, Slimy – zero.

"Second subject!" yelled the magician happily. "Dust!" He said the word gleefully, as if dust was going to be the most fascinating subject.

"No pressure," I told the squish, "But you have to win the next two."

I've got this, he assured me.

"Ugh," Sebille complained. "This subject is going to be dry."

Rustin snickered. "Slimy will really have to dust off some good material."

Lea winked at me. "He'll have to give this subject the white glove treatment."

I groaned. "If bad puns were wings, we could fly right out of here."

The magician jabbed his wand into the air and a chime sounded. He jabbed the wand toward himself. "First strike goes to the Trivia King."

Are you sure? Slimy snarked. *I went first the last time.*

The peanut gallery cheered and clapped just to annoy the magician. It worked like a charm. If only it would put him off his game.

The magician squared his shoulders and pantomimed rolling up his sleeves. He cleared his throat, adjusted his pants, and did a little dance that made him look like a Leprechaun.

"Get on with it!" the peanut gallery hollered.

He grinned our way and cracked his knuckles, dipping forward, he pointed the wand at Slimy. "We'll start with the old tried and true. Dust is a mix of sloughed-off skin cells, hair, clothing fibers, bacteria, dust mites, bits of dead bugs, and soil." He stepped back and did a rooster walk across the stage.

Not so fast, King. The magician's title fell out of Slimy's mouth dripping in acid. *Dust in homes is composed of about 20–50% dead skin cells.*

"Dust is heavy enough to see, and light enough to be carried by the wind," the magician barked out.

Steam therapy is an effective way to remove dust from a respiratory system.

"Woohoo!" we cheered, causing the magician's pale cheeks to redden with pique.

He stabbed the wand at us. "Dust exists in outer space. Cosmic dust is made up of micro-particles of solid material floating around in the space between the stars."

"Boo!" we hissed.

The word "dust" doesn't mean dirty. It means tiny, Slimy exclaimed. The frog gave a satisfied little hop.

The magician stared open-mouthed at Slimy for a beat and then jabbed his wand in our direction. "Dust particles cause light scattering that's responsible for optical events like the color of the sky and halos."

A soft groan filled the room. The magician had scored a hit.

Dust devils are dust-filled vortices that are created when the surface is heated. They're generally smaller and less intense than a tornado.

"Woohoo!!!" We jumped up and down, sure Slimy had won the round.

The magician's face turned deep red, his bushy brows lowering over small eyes. He lifted his wand and jabbed it toward the scoreboard. The numbers on the board changed and we bellowed our outrage.

"Trivia King – two, Slimy – still zero"

The game was rigged. There was no way we'd win.

The magician held up his hands to silence us. "It looks bad for the visiting team. I understand your frustration. But I'm a fair man. The next round will count triple for the winner." His sly smile as we cheered didn't give me a warm and fuzzy feeling. I also had an uncomfortable feeling about the subject of the third round. The Universe knew about Tildy. It wouldn't have chosen that subject unless it had an ace up its sleeve. Something was leaky in Denmark. Or...whatever.

"Subject three. Time-Traveling Tortoises." The magician jabbed the wand at Slimy. "First strike goes to the frog."

Time-traveling tortoises travel across time and space, backward, forward, and sideways.

We clapped.

The magician pointed the wand at Slimy. "TTT are limited in their locomotion by the runes and colors painted on their shells."

Slimy gave an excited little hop. *The Abracadabos Giant Tortoises from the Cayman Islands are extremely rare. There are currently only two known tortoises, named Tildy and Milly. They're sisters.*

We whooped and hollered.

The magician stared blankly at the frog, clearly at a loss. Slimy didn't wait for him to counter.

Tildy and Milly are distant relatives of the Aldabra giant tortoises from the Seychelles near the east coast of Africa.

"Yeeha!!!" I screamed.

Slimy went in for the kill. *The tortoises have been hidden away for decades because they're subject to abuse by unscrupulous magic users.*

The magician's lips curled. I was pretty sure he growled.

They are unregistered magical artifacts and as greatly prized as they are feared for their magic.

"Go Slimy!"

Their mobility is controlled by a clicker that the turtle handler must keep handy at all times.

The Trivia King finally held up a hand. His eyes swirled with rage and his body trembled beneath it.

Grym pointed to the scoreboard. "Time to update the board. Trivia King – two, Slimy – Three. We win."

The magician nodded and I let hope fill my chest. He walked toward the cage holding Wicked, Vel, and Hobs and stared at it a moment, his hands clasped behind his back. Then he turned back to us and he was wearing an evil smile.

My stomach went kerplunk.

He laughed. "You don't think we were unaware of your association with the TTT, do you? We are, of course. And we're also aware that your trivia frog broke the rules."

"What rules?" Rustin yelled.

The magician waved his wand and words began to scroll across the space between us. Tiny, tiny words that were impossible to read. His smile widened. "He didn't wait for his opponent to respond between trivia tidbits. It's in the fine print, of course." He shook his head, sliding an oily glance over Sebille and me. "I'd think you two would have learned your lesson about reading the fine print with the ogre king," he said, bursting into laughter.

We stiffened. He was right about that. Sebille and I had almost had to marry a couple of ogres when we'd engaged a contract with King Rhorr without reading the fine print. Of course, in our defense, the contract was written on the ogre king's back, and the fine print...well...let's just say it dipped into unfriendly territory.

When tall hat wound down a moment later, he wiped fake tears from beneath his eyes. "So, that is that." He jabbed his wand at the board. "I win it all. You lose everything." On the tail of those words, the magician jabbed the air and magic slammed into us, the once-delightful motes of energy melding together to create a multi-hued tsunami of deadly magic.

Vel, Hobs, and Wicked flew from the stage and we were all swept backward, slamming into the wall hard enough to crack bones and expel the air from our lungs. Agony speared my back as I fought the pressing magic, feeling as if my entire body was compressing beneath its power.

In the blink of an eye, the plan we'd cobbled together to get the rune key to save the fairies, as well as the safety of everyone I loved, were blown completely beyond my reach.

16

ABOUT TO BECOME CHIMERA
KIBBLE

Growling with effort, Rustin burst into his chimera form, fighting to peel himself from the wall.

Grym also exploded into his mythical form, his gargoyle several times stronger and harder to control than his human form.

His skinny body bashing into the wall and then bouncing away, only to slam into it again, Hobs gave a high-pitched scream that somehow managed to cut through the thunderous din like a warrior's cry. "Again!" the tiny hobgoblin yelled happily. "Again, again, again!"

A magical web formed in front of Lea. Her face contorted as she tried to push the magic past the compressing energy of the magician's power.

Sebille had burst into her sprite form, her hands outstretched and her eyes squinted mostly shut in an attempt to see beyond the attacking energy. Her power spun before her, unable to move past the wall of power to reach its target.

Eddie stood silently beside me. Too quiet. Too unflappable. I feared he was building his magic again. Chaos would likely help us defeat the magician. But at what cost?

It turned out Eddie's plans weren't the most important consideration at that moment.

With a terrifying roar, Rustin managed to break free of the restraining force. He leaped into the air, his powerful wings pounding the air and carrying him toward the stage.

The magician didn't notice the chimera until it was too late. Rustin was nearly on top of him. Mere inches away. His enormous teeth bared and shiny with anticipatory saliva. The huge paws stretched toward the Trivia King, claws curved and glistening in the light from the sign flashing at the back of the stage.

The magician was about to become chimera kibble.

"No!" I screamed.

"Stop!" Eddie bellowed.

WOOF!!

Magic slammed into me in a heated wave. Familiar magic. Comforting magic.

The world hesitated for a beat, the air stilling and growing solid around me. I blinked, the motion excruciatingly slow as I tried to take in my surroundings.

Sebille was in the air, her iridescent purple and green butterfly wings barely moving as she fought time and space to reach the magician. Her sharp features were set in a glower that didn't fare well for the nasty Trivia King.

Lea's magic web was waving on the air in front of her, moving forward in micro-inches that ensured we'd all be ancient before it arrived to help.

Eddie's eyes were a fractured mishmash of color and shape, the first impetus of his chaotic energy showing in the artificially slowed movement.

Hobs hung in the air, three feet off the ground, his

spidery fingers slowly kneading the nothingness keeping him in place.

Grym had a snarl on his gargoyle face, so like his own but just a little more roughly hewn, his cheeks and jaw sharp like the edges of a rock. His oversized fists were tightly clenched, one foot off the ground and ever so slowly sliding downward in the first of several steps that would take him to the magician.

I pulled air into my lungs and the world suddenly shifted again, softening around me. The foot I hadn't realized I'd lifted, hit the ground and I stumbled forward, barely managing to stay on my feet.

"Woof!" Vel said, tail wagging.

"Good job," I told the little green dog. "Good girl." I gave her a quick scratch behind the ears and glanced around, ensuring that everyone else was still caught in Vel's strange magic. Then I straightened, pulling the pack off my back. I rummaged around inside until my fingers encountered a small, hard object in a rectangular shape. I pulled the prison box from the bag and sent a thin stream of keeper magic into it. A small door appeared on one side.

"In you go," I told the reprehensible magician, holding it close enough for the magic to take hold. The man's form quivered, lengthened, and condensed, oozing through the small door like a stream of smoke and disappearing inside. The door closed and I sighed. "You can let them go," I told my dog.

Vel stood up, licked her lips and shook her head.

Chaos returned.

A roar shook the vault as the chimera's massive paws hit the ground where the magician had stood. Too late, I found myself face to furry muzzle with the dragon slash lion, instantly regretting all my life choices.

Smoke and heat wafted from Rustin's terrifying maw as he roared again, spewing smoky monster breath into my face.

I held my ground, my eyes as big as saucers, and waited for Rustin's brain to reassimilate itself inside the mythical beast.

Another roar blew my hair back off my face, and left it damp with spittle.

Lea's magic web finally arrived, hitting the creature standing in the spot where the magician had been and confining the beast inside gossamer threads of magic that had the strength of steel.

The chimera roared again, thrashing violently in an attempt to escape.

Sebille buzzed over and hit Rustin between the eyes with a sleep spell. He stiffened, gave one last smoke-laced chuff, and then toppled over, snoring like a troll.

My gaze shot to Eddie as the air started to spin with colors. I stabbed a finger in his direction. "Don't."

He jerked, closing his eyes and visibly fighting for control. A moment later he opened them again and they were clear of magic.

Silence filled the room, only the soft sound of panting... me...and Rustin's occasional snore interrupted it.

I took a deep breath and slowly released it before clearing my throat. "Well. That was fun."

Lea snorted. Sebille rolled her eyes. Hard.

I totally won, said the frog. *I'm the Trivia King.*

I banished the snarky response dancing on my tongue. Mr. Slimy had done good work in a frustratingly unwinnable battle. "He had to cheat to beat you. Nicely done," I told the frog. His fat little form stretched with pride and his throat worked more quickly as he digested the praise.

"Let's keep going," Hobs said, his gaze wide with delight. "This place is fun."

"Yeah," I mumbled. "Fun."

"So. How do we get to the next stage?" Lea asked.

We all looked around for another door. There wasn't one. Even the door we'd entered through was gone. *Oh, oh.*

"Meow."

We all turned to find Wicked standing in front of an arched doorway at the side of the room.

"Was that there before?" Lea asked, frowning.

"I don't think so," I responded.

"I really hate to admit it, but that rodent-router has serious door mojo," Sebille grumbled.

"Whatever it is, we'll take it," Eddie agreed.

"What...happened?" a husky voice asked from near the stage.

We all turned to find Rustin trying to cover his exposed dangly bits. His dark hair stuck straight up like he'd sucked an electric bulb and he had a beard.

I blinked. "You have hair on your face."

He frowned. "A side effect of my shift." He looked confused. "Did I?"

"Did you what?" Eddie asked.

"Shift?"

"You did," I said on a sigh.

He looked horrified. "I didn't hurt anybody?"

"No. Lea threw a net on you." I didn't see the point in telling him the net had been meant for the magician. "Get some clothes on and we'll get going. I was thanking the goddess at that moment Grym had insisted the shifters bring extra clothes. Just in case.

"Where's the magician?" Eddie asked, a suspicious glint in his eye.

"I didn't gack him, if that's what you're worried about," I said.

Sebille snorted.

"I might be worried about that if I knew what it was," my brother retorted with a frown.

"He's alive," I said, pointing to the box I'd left on the stage. "He'll be as good as new when the Council releases him." *Unfortunately*.

Eddie nodded. "Good. Nicely done."

Like Slimy, I wasn't immune to a little praise myself. Goddess knew I didn't get much of it. Not that it slowed me down much. But the occasional "atta girl" was good for the soul.

Rustin put on some sweats and, still looking a little foggy, joined us as we all headed through Wicked's door to our next nightmare.

Dave.

17

DAVE

The passageway was cold and wet, the rough rock walls stained with rust where rivulets of water continually seeped over their surface. The space smelled of mildew and rotting vegetation, and the dankness seeped into my bones with icy fingers. We seemed to be climbing down into the center of the earth. The passage narrowed steadily, until the moist rock walls were mere inches from my shoulders. I forced myself to walk directly down the center, arms pressed against my sides, so I could uphold the thin pretense that the slimy walls weren't closing in on me.

My heart pounded as the passage narrowed. My skin turned clammy with sweat.

My footsteps slowed the deeper we went. At some point, my lungs started to tighten, until my breathing turned wheezy.

Fine tremors slipped beneath my skin, my muscles tight and painful.

Every step forward was an exercise in desperation, and

every step away from the door above, a leap of faith I didn't think I'd survive.

At some point along the way, the soft shuffle of tiny foot-steps accompanied our silent passage. The strident squeaks of something I didn't want to encounter carried me to the edge of sanity. Once or twice, I was sure I felt something scurrying over my foot and gave a breathless little yelp, only to discover I'd imagined it.

A quick glance around told me my companions were similarly affected. Even Hobs was subdued, a state I didn't think I'd ever seen the little hobgoblin embrace.

Wicked walked so close to my ankles I stumbled over him more than once. The fat squish had debunked to Sebille's pocket, abandoning his perch on her bony shoulder for the sweet relief of hiding and denial.

I thought about our next challenge. Dave. What could a guy named Dave have for us that would be so terrible? Then I realized I was living what Dave had for us. I was in an emotional prison of foreboding and doubt and dread.

And it was only going to get worse.

Archie's words came flooding back to me. "*His magic taps into your emotions and creates situations that confuse, terrorize, and imprison. Ugly stuff.*"

I twitched, my eyes going wide. Reaching up, I touched Grym on a rock-hard shoulder. If anyone should feel safe in a rocky underground passage, it would be the gargoyle. "How are you?" I whispered to my boyfriend. For some reason, speaking aloud seemed too dangerous an action at that moment. As if I feared what it would draw toward us.

Grym's large body trembled, making my heart stutter in my chest. "Grym?" My voice echoed around the passage and burst into an explosion of sound ahead of us. A beat later, we stepped into a cavern. There was a large, jagged opening at the other end of the cavern, with the view of a large body of water beyond. Whitecaps broke against the sand in foamy ribbons, retreating and swelling in a predictable rhythm. Grym jolted to a stop, his eyes wide with fear.

I walked around him. "What is it? What's wrong?"

He shook his head, stepping backward. He looked as if he was going to bolt back up the passage at any moment.

"Grym, tell me what's wrong." I demanded.

He shook his head, his eyes like saucers. "We have to get out of here."

"Why?" Rustin asked, observing Grym carefully. "What do you see?"

"I don't like water," Grym growled out. "I tend to..." His handsome face flushed with embarrassment. "I sink."

Understanding filled me. Of course he wouldn't like water. As a gargoyle, he was dense and heavy like rock. He'd go straight to the bottom and have trouble getting up again. "But you're not in your gargoyle form anymore."

He shook his head again. "It doesn't matter. I sink."

The sound of splashing water grew, the resonance going from soft and pleasant to louder and more aggressive. I flicked the incoming water a look and felt mildly alarmed. "Is that water closer than it was a second ago?"

"It is," Lea said. "The tide is coming in. Maybe Grym's right. We should get to higher ground."

"I don't think..." Eddie started to say.

His words were drowned out by the thunderous roar of water slamming into the sand mere feet from where we stood. What we were seeing was no normal progression of a rising tide. We were dealing with a magical event.

The water rushed away and shifted back, a wave of foamy water slamming down mere inches from our feet. Without warning, the treacherous wave grabbed Hobs' oversized feet and yanked him to the ground, reeling him in like a fish on a hook.

"Miss!" he screamed, his skinny arms flailing in panic.

In the blink of an eye, he was under the water, and I was screaming his name as I plunged into the frothing surf in search of him.

Whomp! Something punched my shins as the water slammed into me. It snaked around my ankles and yanked me down. "Ahh!" I screamed, the last part of my shriek turning to a gurgle as the water rolled over me. All exterior sound was washed away, leaving only the swell and swish of the water and a muffled gurgle of a scream, which I recognized as Hobs. I forced my eyes to open, the salt stinging painfully as I strained to see the hobgoblin. He wasn't far away. His skinny form was thrashing against the water that continued to drag him away from the shore.

Another large form crashed into the water and slammed into me. A big hand, fingers frantically grasping, grabbed my arm, yanking me close. Grym looked into my face with a terror that threatened to rob me of what little breath I had left. He jerked his head to the side and nodded, then shoved me toward what I assumed was the shore.

I came up spluttering a beat later, hands grabbing for my arms and pulling me free. I grabbed Eddie's hand. "Hobs...!" I couldn't finish my thought, succumbing to a violent coughing fit.

Eddie pulled me back toward the passage, where I saw Lea huddling with Wicked and Vel. "Rustin went in after him. He'll get him, sis. Don't worry."

I nodded, relief replacing a bit of the panic. Then my fear skyrocketed again. "Grym?"

Eddie frowned, glancing behind me as realization filled his expression. "He didn't come out of the water after you?"

My brother tugged me away from the violently grasping water, pushing me gently toward Lea. "I'll get him."

I was already heading back to the water. "We have to hurry. He's been in there a long time."

"Naida!" Eddie yelled. "Get away..."

The water snaked out and grabbed my leg. I started to go down. Eddie grabbed me and pulled, nearly managing to yank me free. Another wave thundered against the small ribbon of remaining sand and I was snatched right out of Eddie's grip.

I went under again, arms and legs flailing against the pressure of the unnatural water. My thrashing hand touched warm flesh and I grabbed Grym's hand. Wrapping my arms around his waist, I kicked hard, using the natural retreat of the water to make headway against its pull. My toes found sand and I kicked hard, somehow managing to drag Grym a few inches with me.

The water thundered over us again. I dug my toes into the bottom as deeply as I could, but was still dragged back several inches.

Despair fought for resolve in my psyche. If it had just been me, I might have just given up. I was so tired, and the force I was battling was so much stronger than I was, it seemed hopeless. But Grym needed me. He'd faced his terror to come in and rescue me, and I wasn't going to let him die as a result.

The water receded and I dug both feet into the sand, pushing and forcing us forward with every bit of strength left in my limbs.

My toes slipped. I felt the minute shift in the water that told me we were about to get pounded again. My calves were screaming. My lungs ached. Despair was working hard to beat out determination in my mind.

The water crashed over us. But before it could pull us back, two sets of hands found us and yanked hard.

Grym and I slid out of the surf and kept going as Adrenaline kicked in and gave Rustin and Eddie the power to pull us away.

"Get clear!" Eddie yelled as he and Rustin supported Grym under the arms and started fast-walking him back toward dry land.

"Hobs?" I asked, I wasn't leaving him in the water.

"Already safe," Rustin yelled. "Come on, Naida!"

I didn't argue. The water was swelling toward me again and there was no way I was letting it pull me down. I ran, ignoring the knives slicing through my calves and the heaving breaths that stabbed my chest.

We didn't stop at the opening to the passage but kept running until the water was a distant drone. Then we collapsed to the ground, our chests heaving with fear and exhaustion.

"Now what?" Sebille asked. I glanced at the sprite, finding her too pale. The constellation of her freckles stood out against the unnatural paleness of her face.

Hobs wrapped his long legs and arms around me and pressed his face into my neck. Tears burned my eyes as I clutched him with a desperation I'd never felt before. "I thought you were gone," I whispered to the little hobgoblin. "I was so scared."

"You went in after me," he breathed. "Nobody's ever done anything like that for me before, Miss. I love you."

"I love you too, buddy." Tears burned salty tracks down my icy cheeks. I bit back a sob, filling my lungs with air and slowly releasing it until my feelings were under control. There would be time to deal with the emotions later. We needed to finish the job in Nom and get back to Enchanted.

My heart swelled at the idea of returning to Croakies bookstore and the artifact library.

Home.

"We need to get out of here," Lea said, her voice slightly strangled. I looked at her and realized she was in the midst of a panic attack. "Lea?"

She shook her head. "It's just..." She covered her mouth with a shaky hand. "The passage isn't there anymore."

"What?" Eddie's head jerked around and he swore softly.

I followed his line of sight, my hopes for a return home growing more distant by the minute.

Lea was right. There was no passage. We couldn't go up, and we couldn't go down. We were stuck in a doorless, windowless, rock prison that was barely big enough to hold all of us.

There was no way out.

A frantic sob exploded from my friend. Her eyes skimmed from side to side with growing panic. I realized watching her that she was more scared even than the situation warranted. My level-headed friend appeared to be suffering a claustrophobia-induced panic attack.

I closed my eyes as emotion swept through me. We needed to find a way out before Lea's fear fractured her mind. "What are our options for getting out of here?" I asked.

"Woof!" Vel offered, looking as if she didn't have a care in the world.

I shook my head. "No, girl. Not a good idea." The last thing we needed was the demon dog bringing the rock walls down on our heads with her special kind of magic.

Eddie leaned against the wall, frowning. "I can do a focused chaos blast to break us out."

"We don't know how thick these walls are," Sebille said.

"And there's no place in here to take cover if it gets wild and wooly."

"I can maybe blast my way through as the chimera," Rustin offered.

A resounding chorus of no's made Rustin step back.

"No offense man," Grym said. "But nobody wants to be in close quarters with that thing."

Rustin sighed. "Point taken."

I looked at Sebille. "Anything?"

She frowned. "You know this is all illusion, right?"

"That illusion felt pretty real back there," Grym growled.

She nodded. "I know. The problem is, I think this is reality magic. The more we believe it's real, the realer it becomes."

"I'm not sure what we can do about that?" I said. "Dave, the AI construct appears to be able to see our greatest fears and use them against us. There's no way we're going to get all of us on the same page to disbelieve any situation."

"I might be able to help with that," Sebille said.

"How?" Lea asked, her voice strangled. Her long, light brown hair was stringy and damp, her jeans and shirt were dirty and torn. I'd never seen the tidy earth witch so disheveled. But none of that even compared to the haunted look tightening her attractive features. "I've been trying to think of a spell and I'm drawing a blank."

Sebille nodded. "It's not a spell to get us to disbelieve the reality of these situations that goddess-be-danged Dave keeps putting us in. Not exactly. It's more a case of...well... not caring."

We all stared at her.

She lifted her hands. "Give me a minute to explain before you start pummeling me about the head and shoulders."

Eddie snickered.

"I'm proposing a hex that temporarily stops us from caring about reality. If we don't get emotional, the AI's tricks won't work on us. Right?"

I thought about that for a minute. It seemed logical. I looked around the group, my gaze stopping on Lea. As a witch, she would know if that could work.

She caught my eye and frowned. "It might work. Without emotions, we aren't in danger of falling for emotive magic. But I see a potential pitfall. We'll essentially be sociopaths for the length of the spell. There's nothing to keep us from hurting each other."

Silence fell over the group...a silence that was finally broken by Wicked batting at the wall, his tail snapping with irritation. Vel joined him there, snuffling around the dirt at the base of the rocky partition.

Lea's gaze snapped up to mine. "Wicked!"

I narrowed my gaze on her. "Are you calling me names or trying to tell me something about my cat?"

She smiled. "Animals aren't susceptible to emotive magic. They're too centered in the natural world, with no anticipation or fear of the future. Wicked, Slimy, and Vel won't be affected by a hex that subdues the caring part of the brain. With his innate magical capabilities Wicked can police our behavior if we get out of hand."

I looked at my cat. He'd stopped batting at the wall and had fixed his orange eyes on me. "Are you up for that, little man?"

Wicked meowed, curling himself around my calves in a figure eight and purring. "I'll take that as a yes," I told Lea.

"Okay," Sebille said. "Lea and I will get started on the hex. It will take us a few minutes. Then, hopefully, we'll get to the end of this final stage of the journey."

I liked the sound of that. More importantly, with a spell to formulate that required a lot of thought and discussion, Lea was distracted from her fear.

Bonus.

I only hoped the rampant terror of what we were proposing didn't show on my own face. Because, I really wasn't looking forward to a situation where my powerful friends lost their humanity in a dangerous, tension-fraught situation.

18

I'M KIND OF BUSY RIGHT NOW, CAT

W e stood in a circle, the animals and Hobs in the center between us. Sebille and Lea had both drawn a spell, aware that neither could hex themselves. As the spell was cast, and the smell of freshly mown grass and spicy herbs slipped over us, I found myself praying to the goddess that we weren't making a horrible mistake. We'd decided we'd have to stay without feeling until we found the key. The minute we regained our emotions, Dave could use his emotive magic against us.

It was going to be a tightrope walk with deadly possibilities.

Then all worry slipped away. Along with all feelings of love or affection. All fear. And, the rocky prison we'd been cast into through our emotional weakness just sifted away.

We found ourselves standing in a room that looked much like a corporate office, with cubicles as far as the eye could see. Every cubicle held a gray metal desk. And every desk held a computer. The computers were old, consisting of clunky monitors and oversized boxes beneath the desks. And playing across each screen was some version of everything we'd encountered since entering the third phase. I slid my gaze over the scenes of endless underground passages, sucking killer water, and claustrophobia-inducing small places. The pictures didn't bother me. I scanned my gaze over them and the scenes we'd managed to avoid without emotion or care.

The computers played out hundreds of equally horrendous potential situations we might have faced if we hadn't found our way out. Monsters threatened to rip off our limbs, we were trapped in a burning house with fire raging around us, lightning snapped at us as we ran, a pack of hungry werewolves chased us toward a cliff, and on and on.

None of it even raised my pulse. There was definitely something to be said for losing the ability to care.

"Welcome," said a voice that seemed too high-pitched to belong to a guy.

I turned to find a slight man with a receding hairline and heavy, black-rimmed glasses striding toward us through the cubicles.

The man wore wrinkled tan pants and a blue button-down shirt that had a mustard stain on the pocket as if he'd jammed a hotdog into it.

He wasn't homely or attractive, but rather non-descript. If I turned my head and looked away, I was sure I'd forget what he looked like.

The man offered a small, pale hand with dark hairs curling from the knuckles as he approached. "I'm the office manager…"

"Dave," we all said before he could.

Wicked spit at the man and Dave looked down on my cat, his non-descript form blurring and pixilating as he appraised my hostile feline. "Ah, a cat." He grimaced. "I'm not fond of the beasts. I'm sure you've met our resident feline? Nasty piece of work."

I shrugged, feeling no need to defend my cat.

Dave's gaze slid to Vel and he blinked. "A demon dog?" He glanced at me. "How did you manage that?"

I shrugged again. "We've come for the rune key. If you'll just show us where it is, we'll steal it and get out of your hair."

"I can't allow you to steal the key," Dave said, his tone petulant.

Hobs wandered away from us and I let him. I didn't care where he was going or what he was going to do. Vel trotted along at his heels.

"You really don't have a choice, Rustin said. "Either you give it to us or we'll take this vault down."

Oh, oh, that tiny voice in my mind said. *We aren't supposed to hurt the vault or its inhabitants,* the voice whined.

The problem was, I didn't really care.

Dave sputtered and huffed. Then, shoving the black glasses up his nose, he slipped into the nearest cubicle, dropped into the chair, and began to create a scenario.

I sighed, glancing at Eddie. "Do your thing. But try to keep the AI intact so he can tell us where the key is."

Eddie's eyes started to fracture into shapes and colors. I looked away, not even curious about what he'd do with his magic. Instead, I checked my watch and sighed. We'd been inside the vault way too long. We needed to get on our way before the Universal Council sent someone to interfere. I was hungry. I didn't want to have to take down a bunch of soldiers before I had lunch. It would be tedious. I looked at Sebille. "Give me a donut."

She shook her head. "I ate them already."

My fists clenched. "You ate *all* the donuts?"

She rounded on me, magic spitting at her fingertips. "I did. Do you have a problem with that?"

Wicked circled my ankles, purring, and thoughts of taking out Sebille and the Universe's soldiers slipped away, leaving a strange numbness behind.

I only wished the numbness would spread to my stomach so I could stop thinking about how hungry I was.

The cubicle in front of me started to shake, chunks of it flying off and spinning around the room. It only took a few minutes before the entire cubicle was fractured into a thousand tiny pieces and the computer was starting to pull apart.

Dave worked more feverishly as the cubicles around him came apart, ducking when he could, and sustaining cuts where he couldn't. Dave's cuts exposed wires and chips instead of blood, but his form flickered and pixilated with every strike.

"This is taking too long," Sebille groused, magic spitting at her fingertips. She eyed Dave and lifted her hand, clearly intending to hit him with a magic whammy.

Wicked rubbed up against her calves, purring even louder than before. She grimaced down at him, but the magic at her fingertips died.

Dave hit the *Enter* button and stood, a smug smile on his forgettable face. "There. That should take care of this little problem."

Why did I think the "little problem" was us?

"What did you do?" Lea asked, looking around without apparent concern.

"You'll see," Dave answered, crossing his arms over his chest.

The room spun and roiled with chunks of cubicle, desk, chair, and computer. The air was so thick with debris, even we weren't safe from the chaos any longer.

"Give that a rest," I told Eddie. "It's not making a difference anyway. We're going to have to get more physical."

Eddie threw me a scowl and ignored me. In fact, with a wave of his hand, he turned up the burners on the flying debris, spurring it to dangerous levels of activity.

Hunks of plastic crashed through the windows on the outside wall, uncovering concrete where the fake windows had been.

Dave yelped and ducked as a big piece of glass from the front of a computer sliced through his arm, ripping faux flesh and causing more wires and chips to be exposed. He eyed the damage, a tiny pair of tweezers appearing in his hand as he tried to repair the breach.

He nearly pixilated apart for a beat and then tweaked something in the rupture and turned solid again. Dave's brows lifted and he glanced at the big, round clock on the wall.

A beat later, a door marked, "Restroom" opened on the back wall and something with horns and hooves bashed its way through. The thing, which looked like a bull only much bigger, ripped the door frame and the wall away to make room for its prodigious bulk. It stopped in the center aisle and pawed the ground, its eyes red and its large, curved horns gleaming with menace.

We all looked at the thing, then turned to Rustin.

"You're up," I told him.

Without a thought, he burst into his chimera form and roared, fire bathing the air in front of him.

The bull bellowed, its nostrils flaring as it lowered its enormous head and charged.

Rustin charged too.

I watched the impact, surprised that the chimera

managed to avoid the deadly horns and impressed the bull didn't seem affected by the chimera's fire.

The two massive creatures crashed into cubicles, slammed into walls and ignored the increasingly chaotic minefield of sharp parts clogging the air.

A hunk of chair slammed into me, taking me to the ground. I shoved upright, trying to see why my leg hurt so badly, and found a long piece of wood sticking out of my calf. "Eddie, I told you to stop."

"I have no intention of stopping until Dave gives us the key."

A plaster vase slammed into Lea's head and she went down. As she fell, she threw fire at Eddie, igniting his hair.

He calmly yanked the fire from his head and threw it into the chaos, adding a new level of deadly to the maelstrom.

Dave handily ducked the first finger of flame but stepped right into the path of another. Fire caught his cotton shirt and flared brightly, hungry for the highly flammable material. Dave sighed, tapped a couple of keys on the nearest computer, and the sprinkler system came on.

Water rained down on everything and everyone in the room.

The bull flew through the air and slammed into a window. The glass shattered but the beast managed to keep his feet. He charged back toward Rustin, who was biting at the chunks of office furniture flying around his head.

The bull crashed into Rustin and they soared across the room, crashing into a glass-fronted office that I assumed belonged to Dave.

Even in my benumbed state, I knew things were getting out of hand.

"Meow," said my cat. I looked down just as Wicked leaped off the ground, landing in my arms.

I eyed him. "I'm kind of busy right now, cat..."

Wicked unleashed his claws and smacked me on the cheek.

"Ow!" the numbness washed away and my emotions came crashing back." I blinked for a beat, feeling as if I'd been body-slammed by the red-eyed bull. My senses slowly returned, though, and I looked around me with a new perspective. "Holy pork rinds on a pickle." I looked over to find Sebille and Lea strangling each other, their clothing torn and blood running from assorted cuts on their faces and arms.

Eddie was happily stirring the chaos pot, but I saw a tightness in his face that told me he was magically overextending himself.

Grym... "Where's Grym?"

Wicked yowled, heading toward the sprite and the witch.

"Right. I need to find Hobs and Vel too." I hurried along the open area in front of Dave's shattered office and ducked into a door that said, "Supplies".

There were no supplies inside the room, but there were a series of backdrops that I realized probably formed the basis of our nightmare scenarios from before.

Somewhere in the distance, I heard Hobs' excited voice. I followed the sound past a slimy-walled, too-narrow rock passage. And past a cavern with waves pounding against the shore. There was a volcano spewing red-hot lava. A forest that was engulfed in flame. And several equally terrifying scenes, including a plane filled with passengers that was plunging toward the ground.

Shuddering at the thought of living through any of the

scenarios, I turned a corner and found my missing peeps. They were hurrying toward me, and behind them was a huge room with what looked like acres of empty metal shelving.

"Miss! We found the key."

Vel barked excitedly and Grym held up a small black box.

"How'd you find it?" I asked.

"I'm not sure, actually," he pointed toward the room with the shelves. "We stepped into that room. It was filled with shelves upon shelves of things, sort of like at Croakies. But as I approached the shelves, everything shimmered away and this box was all that was left behind. It was like the vault knew why we'd come and, since we'd beaten the challenges, it just handed it over."

"While protecting everything else in the vault." I nodded, putting out my hand. Grym handed the box to me and I opened it, gasping in surprise.

"You need to hurry, Naida," Grym said. "It sounds like they're pulling the vault down around our ears."

I nodded, dropping to my knees and pulling the bag of replication artifact from my pocket. I quickly made a copy of the icon and replaced it in the box, handing the original back to Grym. As he ran the box back to the shelves, I slipped the copy into my pocket, along with the replication artifact.

Grym arrived as I straightened and pulled my pack over my shoulders. "Let's go."

As we hurried back, the sounds of crashing, screaming, and bellowing had Grym frowning. "What's going on in there?"

I sighed. "You don't want to know. Suffice it to say, Wicked's got his paws full."

Grym shook his head.

When he pushed the door open into the office, a massive mythological creature was heading right for us. Grym slammed it shut and pushed us aside.

The door quaked under the impact but managed to hold up.

I narrowed my gaze on him. "You're not under the spell anymore."

He smiled. "I touched the key. It stripped the hex from me."

I felt my eyes go wide. I'd known the key could unlock magic, but I hadn't known it could remove it.

We tried the door again and found it safe. Thankfully, Eddie's chaos magic had been extinguished, and Lea and Sebille had stopped trying to throttle each other. But poor Wicked was having trouble reaching the chimera to return Rustin's conscience to him.

Grym flashed into his gargoyle form and marched over to the bull. As the rampaging fiend started to turn his way, Grym punched it in the side of the head. It went cross-eyed, wobbled, and then hit the ground, unconscious.

Caught in mid-attack, the chimera sent a wave of flame in the gargoyle's direction. Grym ducked the fire and started forward again, his fist clenched for another punch.

Rustin roared, but before the chimera could attack Grym, Wicked ran over and slashed his claws across a beefy foreleg. The beast roared its rage at the attack, then stopped, blinked a few times, and shrunk down to Rustin on a flash of light.

Silence permeated the office. I looked around and all the blood left my face at the mess. Dizziness claimed me for a beat. There wasn't a single piece of intact furniture in the place. Every wall had been punched through in several places, and Dave was covered in cuts and scratches.

So much for *do no harm*.

The AI construct stood where I'd left him, his form flashing and pixilating as if he were about to shut down. As I watched, he slowly shoved his glasses up his nose. "The Council guard will be here shortly. You will pay for this destruction." And then he blipped into nothingness, leaving only the stench of an overheated computer behind.

19

TELL HOBS I NEED A DISTRACTION

"We need to get out of here," Eddie said. "If the guard gets hold of us, we'll be tied up here for hours. Maybe days."

"How do we get out?" Lea asked.

"Back the way we came," Rustin offered.

I cringed at the idea, but knew he was right. We'd run the gauntlet in and we'd need to run it out.

We ran back to the spot where we'd entered the office, the space around us changing in the blink of an eye from corporate office to underground cavern. We kept a wide berth between us and the water and hit the passage, never slowing as we ascended back toward the Trivia King's space.

All was quiet in the magician's realm. His prison box still sat near the edge of the stage, and the lighted sign above the platform still flashed his faux fame.

We hit the door into the Nomook's realm and didn't look up as we ran for the door. To my relief, the entrance door was open and we plunged through.

We ran across the grass to the spot where we'd landed on our arrival. Excitement made me giddy. We were going to make it! I threw down my pack and reached for the Book of Pages in my pocket. My fingers closed around the book.

"Everybody gather around," I instructed. "Hurry."

"Stop right there!" said a hard, angry voice.

I went still, my head slowly lifting. Dozens of black-uniformed guards were arrayed before us, dozens of weapons pointed at our heads.

No, no, no, no, no! It couldn't be.

We'd been too slow, and we'd failed.

The guard who'd spoken was bigger than the rest, broader, with piercing blue eyes and a head of pure white hair that stuck up on top as if he'd been shocked by a few thousand volts of electricity. The guard held out his hand, his smile tight. "Give me the key, Naida keeper. We don't want anybody to get hurt."

I shook my head, clutching it to me and rising. I took a step back and then another.

"Naida," Grym said in a warning voice.

I shook my head again. "I can't let the fairies die."

The guard's gaze softened infinitesimally. I might have missed it entirely if I hadn't been looking directly into his eyes. "We'll see to the fairies," the guard said. But something in his tone of voice told me he was making promises he wasn't sure he could keep.

"You know where they are?"

He stared at me, his silence speaking volumes.

I took another step back, wondering if I could engage the Book of Pages before the guards reached us. I glanced around at my group, willing them with my eyes to come closer.

"Naida."

The female voice emerged from somewhere behind the guards. The sound of it had the guard with the white hair standing a little taller, his posture stiffening. His lips formed a hard line and his gaze on me became a warning.

I had no idea what he was warning me about, but my mind was spinning wildly and I didn't really care in that moment.

I knew that voice.

Eddie stepped up next to me, dropping an arm around my shoulders. In that moment, I knew he'd betrayed us. "No." I shook my head, trying to step away from him.

"It's not what you think," my brother started to say.

I jerked away, coming out from underneath his arm. "How could you do this to us? To Sebille?"

Eddie slid a guilty look toward the sprite, tensing when he saw the murderous look on her long, narrow face. Tears shimmered in her stunning gaze and her slender form was tight with rage. "If she dies, I'll come after you," she whispered softly. "That's a promise."

Eddie flinched as if struck.

A slender woman, five feet nine inches tall, with long, straight blonde hair and hazel eyes stepped out of the lines of guards and stopped next to white hair.

I knew how tall she was and that her eyes glowed with silver energy when she was alarmed or upset. I knew she preferred soft sweaters and long skirts.

I knew she hadn't been a real mother to her daughter for decades.

I knew all that because I knew her.

"What's going on," I asked my mother. "What are you and Eddie up to?"

Narina Griffith settled her hazel gaze on me and smiled, her expression deceptively serene. She glanced at white hair and nodded. He stepped back into the lines of guards and folded his hands, legs wide, watching me like a hawk.

Narina, a.k.a. my mother, stepped closer. She lifted the fingers of her right hand and a brisk wind blew up behind her, cutting us off from the guards audibly but not physically. If I tried to run with the key still clutched in my hand, I had no doubt white hair and his guards would be on us in a heartbeat.

"We won't be overheard," Narina said. She gave me a smile I assumed was meant as an apology, but we were well past that making a difference.

"You can't stop us from doing this," I told her. "Queen Sindra and the fairies will die if we don't intervene."

"Jacob Quilleran can't be allowed to acquire the rune key. It would be catastrophic."

"I know that, mother," I growled. "We weren't going to give him the real thing." I glowered at my brother. "I'm sure Eddie told you that."

My brother shook his head, looking away.

"He did," she admitted, surprising me. "Which was why we already replaced the real key with that fake."

I blinked. "You what?" I looked down at the familiar icon, my heart twisting with remembered pain. When my parents had left me behind to hare off and do whatever they did for most of my life, the family crest resting on my palm had been all that was left to remind me of my family. A family who hadn't cared enough about me to stay and guide me through my life and my magic. It had been woven into the blanket they'd left me wrapped in. It had been on the head of my crib. I still had the blanket with our family crest tucked safely into a trunk at the bottom of my bed, along with an old teapot my mother had left behind when she'd abandoned me. Neither one made any difference, because I'd never felt as if I had a family.

Though, I guessed the fact that I'd held onto them said something.

I stared at the age-tarnished locket, a stylized G with the outline of a heart intersecting the rounded top and a thorny rose whose long stem wove through both. Looking back at our family history, I couldn't help thinking that heart was a mockery...a disgrace...and I suddenly wanted to fling the thing on the ground. Instead, I looked up at my mother. "This isn't the real thing?"

She shook her head, the skin around her eyes, tight. "I'm sorry, Naida." She held out her hand, palm up. "I'll take that now, please."

I smiled. "If this is a fake, why do you care if I keep it?" I reached out to Slimy on our mental communication channel. *Get everybody to me.* I thought about that and corrected my instruction. *Everybody but Eddie. And tell Hobs I need a distraction.*

Your wish is my command, princess bossy.

I barely kept from rolling my eyes. Instead, I refocused on Narina.

At a loss how to answer my question, my mother opened her mouth and then closed it, frowning. "It simply saves me from creating another one," she finally said.

I nodded as if I completely understood. "You don't mind if I make a copy then? I'd love to have this to hang on a chain."

Narina paled. "I don't think..."

A loud cracking sound speared the air, drawing every gaze skyward. The hobgoblin stood on an enormous branch high above our heads, his small face a study in delight as he jumped and waved his arms. "Hi, Miss! Isn't this a great tree?"

I reached into the bag I'd stuffed in my pocket. "That's a

great tree, Hobs." I withdrew my hand and wrapped it around the family crest. "But it sounds like it's breaking. You should come down now."

I grabbed the Book of Pages from my other pocket as my group surrounded me, their expressions perfectly blank. Lea held Wicked and Sebille was holding Vel close.

"All right, Miss!" Hobs leaped into the air, soaring so high he surpassed the top of the giant oak. His acrobatic leap drew a chorus of Ohs and Ahs from the Universal Guard.

"Naida, is he going to be all right?" My mother asked.

The book expanded in the hand I held behind my back. "Hobs," I called out. "Come down here right now."

The little hobgoblin landed, but not on the ground. His oversized feet hit the tree branch and it shifted under a thunderous crack, then a beat later he was falling with the enormous branch, riding it like a surfer as it plummeted toward the ground.

There was a chorus of husky yells as the guards dove out of the way.

The branch hit the ground with a thunderous "Thump!" and shattered, slivers and chunks flying everywhere.

But Hobs was airborne. He landed in Narina's arms with a delighted cackle. "Again!"

My mother stumbled backward, but she wasn't allowed to regain her balance as Hobs pushed off her and flew into Grym's arms.

I threw the icon in my hand to the ground. "Goodbye mother," and slapped my palm onto the book, where a picture of Croakies beckoned us home.

Within a single breath, the magic grabbed us, yanked us off the ground, and sent us spinning, as we were ripped into the pages of the book, and torn away from Nom.

20

A POX UPON YER SPINE

We landed in a tangle of legs and arms, and were immediately greeted by a squeal that came from the back of the bookstore. A small brown blur slammed into Hobs.

Baca hugged him tight. "You're home! I was so worried."

Hobs' eyes were bright with excitement. "We fought a giant three-headed cat and a cheating magician and got lost in a cave and almost drowned. Then we fought a huge bull and exploded a bunch of computers. It was fun!"

Baca clapped her tiny hands. "I'm jealous!"

Hobs laughed and the two of them headed toward the library, Wicked and Vel on their heels.

Rustin begged off, pleading a need to pick up Sadie from Birte's, where she'd spent the hours we were gone.

Lea gave me a hug and followed him out, heading home to feed Hex.

Sebille settled Slimy in his terrarium and turned on his heat lamp. "I'll feed him before I go to bed," she said, looking as weary as I felt.

Grym pulled me into a hug. "Good work, keeper. You got the key and we all came out of it alive and not imprisoned."

"I got a copy of a copy of the key, you mean."

He grinned.

"So far, anyway. I fully expect my mother and traitorous brother to show up on my doorstep in a day or so."

He tapped me on the nose. "If they're smart, they'll wait a few days. I don't think I've ever seen you so mad."

"I don't think I've ever been that mad," I agreed, yawning.

Sebille covered Slimy's home with a blanket and left him with his dinner, a bunch of crickets judging by the chirping. "Are you sure you left the right key behind?" the sprite asked me.

I pulled it out of my pocket and stared at it, rubbing a finger over its surface. Seeing the family crest again made me sad. It was both a reminder of good times and bad. "I did. Not that it really matters..." I handed it to her. "They were both copies." I wondered how long it would take for my mother to figure out we'd left the real key inside the vault. My gaze caught on hers. "You'll take care of loading it up with the right magic?"

She nodded. "I'll see you in the morning." Hesitating at the door, she turned back to me. "Did Archie leave us a note?"

My uncle had told us he'd slip a note through the mail slot if he managed to find the fairies. I glanced that way and saw nothing. "I don't see one. I'll call him in a few minutes."

As the door closed behind Sebille, I leaned into Grym, enjoying his warmth and quiet support. We stood in companionable silence for several minutes, just enjoying the peace and comfort of being home. Then he pulled back. "I'm going home. Call me if you need help."

"I will."

He cupped my face, his dark-caramel gaze holding mine. "Don't go after Jacob Quilleran without me."

"I won't."

"Promise?"

I smiled, holding up a hand as if taking an oath. "You have my word."

His lips met mine and held, gentle and lingering. Heat from his body infused me at the touch, and something delicious swirled in my belly. He broke the kiss way too soon and left, ordering me to lock and ward the door behind him.

I was still smiling when I did as he asked, feeling better than I'd felt in hours.

I dialed Archie and listened to the phone ring several times before giving up. Leaving him a brief message, I disconnected, yawning widely enough to make my jaw creak. I needed to get some sleep. We had to find the fairies and deal with Jacob soon, but it was out of my hands for the moment, and I wouldn't do anybody any good if I was dead on my feet. Flipping off the bookstore light, I opened the dividing door. "Night, Slimy."

Night, Naida.

I hesitated a beat and then added, "You *are* the Trivia King."

Silence met my statement. I pictured the fat squish blinking in surprise. Then, his ever-ready cockiness returned in his response. *Of course. I've been telling you that.*

Despite the copious amount of attitude in his response, I could feel his pleasure at my words. I smiled to myself and stepped through the door, wearily climbing the stairs to my apartment.

With any luck, we'd find the fairies quickly and I could tell Jacob Quilleran to stick it. But it felt good to have a backup plan with the fake key just in case. Because, if I'd learned anything since entering the magical world, it was that nothing was set in stone. And no seeming absolutes could be trusted to stay that way.

The road ahead would be bumpy and likely a hot mess. After all, that was my modus operandi as an artifact keeper. I wouldn't want to confuse anybody by suddenly becoming overly competent.

I TOSSED and turned in fitful dreams, more awake than asleep and working twice as hard than if I'd given up on trying to rest. Images of dark, damp passageways and the threatening thunder of waves on a sandy shore mixed with the silliness of a trivia contest that couldn't be won and pixilating computers shaped like nerds.

By the time I wrenched myself from sleep, panting and sweaty, I knew I wouldn't rest again until Queen Sindra and the fairies were home and safe.

I didn't even care whether her chosen home was the Primordial Forest or Enchanted. I just wanted to know they were all safe. Besides, I told myself as I shuffled wearily to the shower, if they ended up at the forest bordering Illusion City, Sebille and I could visit my friends LA and Deg whenever we visited Sindra. The witch and familiar pair had helped me more than once with the Quilleran crew, and they lived with the rest of Hex and Wicked's littermates. The thought of seeing the cats again made me smile as I turned the water as hot as I could stand, and stepped beneath it.

I was pulling sneakers on when the door to Croakies Bookstore jangled softly in the distance. I glanced at the cat-shaped clock on the wall and worry flared. It would be unusual for Sebille to have gone out for donuts so early. Especially, since she'd have had a late night loading the fake rune key with magic the night before. I knew for sure we were in trouble when I spotted Sebille hurrying across the artifact library to see who'd arrived.

Someone had breached our ward, a considerably complex one developed by none other than Madeline Quilleran. I could count on two fingers the number of people who could breach that ward. Madeline being one of them.

Jacob Quilleran being another.

Sebille's gaze lifted to mine and caught, our matching expressions of dread and worry causing my heart to thunder in my chest.

I held up a finger for her to wait, and I tried dialing my Uncle Archie again. If he'd somehow managed to find the queen since the last time I'd called, our next steps would be different than if he hadn't.

The phone rang and rang and I finally hung up, shaking my head at Sebille.

She took a deep breath, magic spitting at her fingertips, and reached for the handle. By the time I ran down the steps, she was pulling the door open.

I'd thought I was ready for what we would find. I was wrong.

"Hello, dear girl," Uncle Archie said, his voice tight with strain. A quick scan over my uncle's person told a story I didn't like at all. He was wearing his sorcerer's robe, looking like he'd been pulled directly from his office at the Société of Dire Magic. The robe was filthy and tattered, as if he'd been dragged across a field. Dirt also caked his face and covered the once-black boots I saw beneath his robe. His tall, slender form looked even more emaciated than usual, dark hollows filling his usually rosy cheeks.

His curly brown hair was a tangled mess, as if he'd traveled through a wind tunnel, and his blue eyes, so like mine, were haunted and dull with fear.

I had a pretty good idea why he looked scared and I doubted that fear was for himself. It was likely because he knew that the man standing behind him intended to use my affection for Archie against us all.

"Uncle. Are you all right?"

Archie shrugged. "To be honest, I've been better."

I nodded. "I see that."

"Where are my mother and the fairies?" Sebille barked out, the magic around her fingers growing until I worried she'd no longer be able to control it.

Jacob Quilleran feigned surprise. "You know where they are, sprite. They're exactly where you left them two days ago." He cocked his head. "Do you have my key?"

I stared at Archie, willing him to give me a message I could use to make everything okay. His dark eyes narrowed slightly, the skin creasing in the corners, but there was nothing I could read in his expression.

"I want them back," Sebille said. Her hard tone had me turning her way. The sprite's vibrant gaze was too wide, her form too stiff. She was teetering on the edge and I worried what would happen if she fell over it.

I fought the urge to touch her arm in warning. In her current state, she might send all that energy in my direction if I startled her. I'd have to try to diffuse the situation with Jacob if I was going to have any hope of keeping Sebille from blowing us all up.

I looked at the witch. "We did as you asked. We got the rune key. You need to release the fairies."

Jacob extended his hand. "I'll take the key."

I glanced at Sebille. She gave me a small nod.

"Not without proof that the fairies are okay," I told him. We'd discussed what we would do if Jacob demanded the key before releasing Queen Sindra and the others. We'd known it was a strong possibility and didn't trust him the tiniest bit to do as he'd promised once he had the key.

Jacob's jaw tightened. His cruel, icy-blue gaze narrowed. "Are you sure that is the stance you wish to take?"

Something drew my gaze to Archie. His mouth was pressed in a straight line, the creases around his eyes had deepened. I noted the fine trembling in his tall form and it suddenly hit me. Jacob had him under some kind of spell. And from the looks of it, he was in a considerable amount of pain. "What are you doing to him?" I demanded, my own magic flooding to my fingertips. Though my magic wasn't generally useful against magical attacks, there was one exception. Inside of Croakies my power was absolute. And my control over the artifacts under my care was daunting.

With a thought, I lifted every book in the store off the shelves, moving them toward Jacob until he was surrounded. I flicked a finger and the lock on the front door snicked closed, the ward settled into place.

The dividing door blew open and a familiar squawk pierced the early morning silence as a large, noisy tumble-weed of feathers and beak rolled through the air toward me. SB, short for sewer beak, skimmed over Jacob's head and slammed into the wall before righting himself and fluttering around the room spewing the gutter talk he was named for. Fortunately, the keeper before me had doused him with a bleeping spell, so that most of his salty language came out as bleeps. "A curse upon yer barnacled hide. A pox upon yer spine. For Blackbeard's blade will split yer bleep, making way for the sun to shine. Bwawk!" SB did another flyby of Jacob's head, snagging a few strands of the witch's dark hair in his talons as he passed.

Jacob gave an outraged grunt and sent a bolt of magic after the cagey parrot.

The magic sailed harmlessly by as SB went into a surprisingly competent barrel roll, but it painted a wide black mark across my wall.

The air whispered above my head and I threw up my arm just as Blackbeard's sword arrived, smacking into my palm.

Jacob flinched when he saw the sword. He'd been beaten the last time I'd used the artifact against him, and I fully intended to beat him again.

"Release Archie from whatever spell you've put him under," I demanded. My voice reverberated through the room, a nice little twist I'd been practicing lately. It in no way reflected my ability to cause havoc or harm, but it sounded really badapple and I enjoyed using it.

Jacob's response was to reach out and twist his hand, fingers bent as if he were cupping something within them. As he twisted, Archie's legs buckled and he went down hard, crying out as his knees hit the floor.

Sebille flung magic at the witch in a pale green wash, but Jacob threw up an arm and caught it like one would catch a baseball, pinching it away in his fist.

He smiled, slowly twisting again to make Uncle Archie cry out and writhe on the ground.

The sword in my hand sang, infusing me with a nearly uncontrollable desire to fight, and it took everything I had to resist, knowing Archie would be the one to suffer.

"Give me the key, Naida keeper, or your uncle will die."

There was a beat of tense silence while I considered the

situation, and then I opened my hand and let the sword drop to the rug. All the books hit the floor as I dropped my magic. The sound was deafening, alarming, but Archie didn't so much as flinch. He was lost in a private nightmare of pain and manipulation.

"Bwawk! Ye scurvy dog. May yer fleas have fleas and yer bleep have the runs."

I barely registered SB's curse. My heart was breaking just looking at Archie. "Stop hurting him. Let him go."

Jacob turned a smug smile to Sebille. She skewered him with a glare, the magic spitting hungrily above her hand.

"Sebille," I said softly, my voice pleading. "Look at him."

Her hard green gaze slid to Archie and I saw the moment she softened. Her narrow shoulders drooped and she dropped her hand, the magic fizzling away with a soft pop.

"Good. Now, give me the key."

Sebille reluctantly pulled it from her pocket. "How do we know you'll keep your word and bring the fairies back?"

Jacob's laughter was deep, oily with evil. "You don't, of course. But I'm a man of my word. You'll get your mother back, young sprite. As soon as I test this to make sure you haven't given me a fake."

I twitched, ducking my head as his keen gaze slid my way. "You're not trying to get away with fooling me, are you Naida keeper?" He twisted his hand and something on Archie's body cracked. He howled in agony and tears sprang into my eyes. "No!"

The air between us thickened and I jumped as a woman in a long black dress appeared out of thin air. She was nearly as tall as Jacob, with a thick curtain of black hair that fell well past her shoulders, and cheekbones that looked sharp enough to cut paper.

Madeline Quilleran reached out and grabbed the key from Sebille's hand before we had time to react. Then she flicked her other hand and hit Jacob with a wall of magic that flung him backward and slammed him into the door. Before he even hit the ground, she hit him again, the energy pressing him into the thick metal door as if he were a cookie cutter and the metal was her dough.

Jacob bellowed with outrage and pain as his sister approached, the wall of energy emerging from her hand a relentless force that threatened to press him flat.

Madeline spared me a quick glance. "Get your uncle out of here and then come back. You and I have an appointment with the Council."

I shook my head. "The fairies."

Madeline's piercing yellow eyes focused on me, their brilliance hard and unrelenting. "There are things you don't know, Naida keeper. You'll have to trust me to do what is right."

"We don't need to do any such thing," Sebille declared hotly. "You should let us finish what we started. We would have gotten everybody what they wanted."

Madeline laughed, the sound a feminine version of her brother's. She jerked her chin at Jacob. "I don't think you're going to be able to sell the Council on the idea that giving this monster the rune key is a good idea."

Sebille opened her mouth, no doubt to tell Maddie that we weren't actually giving him the real key, but I cleared my throat to keep her quiet. Her gaze shot to me and I widened my eyes.

Fire lit her gaze, fueled by frustration as much as rage.

"We'll talk, Maddie," I said. "Maybe we can come to a compromise."

"I'm thinking magical waterboarding is a good option," Sebille growled.

I bumped Sebille with my arm. "Help me with Archie?"

She nodded, though her expression was anything but pleased by the turn of events. Between us, we got my uncle off the floor and helped him into the artifact library. The dividing door closed, locked and warded, at my command. We stood at the bottom and looked up at the steepness of the flight of stairs leading up to my apartment.

"Meow!" Wicked exclaimed, flying past us to the dividing door. He bumped it with his paw and I said, "It's warded, Wicked. You can't..." The door unlocked and opened just as an explosion rocked the bookstore, and a very feminine scream sliced through the space.

21

WHAT ARE WE TO DO WITH YOU, YOUNG LADY?

We left Archie propped up against the stairs and hurried back out to the bookstore. Madeline lay in the center of the room, a perfect scorched circle surrounding her. All the books that had been inside that space had been blown away to leave a bare space where, as close as I could tell, Jacob had set off one heck of a magic bomb.

Madeline's eyes were open and, she wasn't moving. When I knelt beside her, she groaned, her fingers twitching. Sebille and I helped her sit up. "Where's Jacob?" I asked the witch. "Did he get the key?"

Madeline shoved at a rooster's comb of hair sticking straight up from her face and Sebille snorted. I glared at the sprite, but felt my lips twitching at the sight of perfect Madeline Quilleran sporting a crashin' mohawk, her eyes blinking at us from inside two circles of white surrounded by black soot.

Madeline suddenly seemed to come back to herself. She shoved our helping hands away and sprang to her feet, staring around the bookstore as if she couldn't remember how she'd gotten there.

"Where's your brother?" I tried again. "Did he escape?"

She shook her head and I embraced a moment of hope that she'd somehow contained him. But her words ripped that hope away. "I can't believe he attacked me."

Sebille and I shared a look of disbelief ourselves. I couldn't believe she wouldn't believe Jacob Quilleran capable of just about anything.

"Where did he go?" Sebille asked. "We need to find him. He might go to the fairies. He likely thinks we're working against him now." She scoured Madeline with a glower. "You probably just got my mother killed."

Her words seemed to knock Maddie the rest of the way out of her stupor. She straightened, squaring her shoulders, and looked down her nose at Sebille. The air around her crackled with latent energy and shadows reached for her from every corner of the room.

I took a step back, despite being in the place where my magic was strongest. On my best day, I'd never touch Madeline Quilleran's power level.

"Watch yourself, sprite. You forget you're speaking to a Power That Be. I am a duly elected representative of the Universal Council." She turned to me and I fought the urge to backtrack again. "You!" she said, her eyes snapping with power, "...have been summoned by the Council. You will come with me."

Before her words even had time to sink in, she'd curled her long fingers around my wrist and the shadows tumbled into me, wrapping me in a formless place of silence and magic that felt like cool satin against my skin.

The last thing I heard was Sebille screaming, "Wait!" and then the world seemed to disappear.

I could no longer feel Madeline's grip on my wrist, or see

her next to me. Only the steady, too-rapid thump of my heart warned me that I was still alive. And terrified.

There was a sensation of relocation without movement. I couldn't feel the ground under my feet. And, when I thought about it, I realized I couldn't feel the rest of me either. I couldn't move my head or my limbs. There was only the slightly reassuring, inexorable beating of my heart.

Muffled sounds eased through the nothingness, gradually getting louder.

Voices.

Arguing.

Suddenly my feet were on a firm surface again and the shadows were retreating. I blinked around, my mind trying to understand my surroundings. Everything was still a bit hazy, as if the trip had scrambled my vision.

A chorus of gasps drew me out of my thoughts. For a horrifying minute, I thought Madeline had ripped me right out of my clothes. All my nightmares about showing up at school naked rushed in on me, making me squeak with alarm. But a quick glance down reassured me. And when I looked into the faces of the people arrayed around a long, curved desk across the room, I saw that they were staring at Maddie, not me.

Madeline seemed flustered, a strange sight, since she'd always presented herself as completely competent and self-assured. She touched her face and then her hair. "What...?" Inexplicably, she turned to me, a question in her piercing yellow eyes.

I grimaced. "You have a little something there," I pointed to my face. "And your hair is..." I grimaced again.

Her eyes went wide with horror when she reached up and felt the mohawk she was sporting. With a snap of her fingers, her hair and soot issues disappeared and she was once again perfectly groomed. She gave the people at the front of the room a slight bow. "My apologies, I'm afraid I encountered some problems with my brother."

"He didn't get the key?" a familiar voice asked.

My gaze shot to the woman at the end of the dais. My mother. *Holy step-mother of the goddess's best friend!* Narina Griffith was on the Universal Council? I felt suddenly faint, my knees weakening beneath me.

"Naida!" Narina barked. "Fortify yourself, girl."

I jumped to attention, shocked by the harsh tone my mother had used. My gaze locked onto hers, and I let the caustic mix of emotions I was feeling swim through it. "Well. This explains so many things."

Another gasp. That time it had come from Madeline. "You will not speak to Council members that way, *Keeper*." She all but spat my title, as if I were a flattened piece of dog poo on her shoe.

"Personal issues don't belong in the council chambers," a deep voice said from further down the dais. Mind yourself, Naida keeper."

"Bow," Madeline whispered harshly.

Pulse pounding as I realized the man who'd spoken sat in the middle of the long, curved platform. I was pretty sure that meant he was the lead council member. I reluctantly bowed, knowing I'd already peeved everyone in the room off by not doing it immediately. "I'm sorry, sir, I..."

"Silence!" the man barked. His slightly bulgy brown eyes were wide with outrage. "You will remain silent until spoken to."

I swallowed hard, biting back a response.

The lead council turned to Maddie. "PTB Quilleran, what is your report?"

The witch inclined her head. "Sir, I encountered my

brother, Jacob Quilleran at the artifact library when I arrived to summon the keeper. He attacked me for the key..." she skimmed me a quick, unreadable look. "I was able to gain access to it before he could take it from the KoA. Though, I attempted to subdue him, I'm ashamed to say he got the better of me and escaped."

"And the key?" the man asked.

She reached into a pocket of her dress and produced the fake rune key. My heart skipped a beat as I realized all the work we'd done to get the key would be for nothing. Tears burned my eyes. I blinked them away, determined not to show the self-important boobs around that dais any emotion at all.

Madeline strode to the dais and handed the key to my mother. Narina rubbed a finger over its surface and her lips curved upward in a slight smile. The smile was gone a beat later when she glanced toward the brown-skinned man at the center of the dais and nodded.

"Good. That crisis has been averted then." The man turned his attention on me. I gave him back as blank a face as I could manage. "Now. What are we to do with you, young lady?"

I shrugged. "Hang me from the yardarm? Draw and quarter me."

The faces behind the curved platform registered surprise at my suggestions.

"Why not?" I asked. "I dared to try to save my friends from certain death. Clearly, I'm a monster of the worst kind."

"Naida," my mother warned.

I swung around, my patience gone. "No. You don't get to lecture or reprimand me. You deserted me when I was little more than a baby. Just walked away. Why?" I lifted my hands and swung them around. "For power? Prestige?" I shook my head. "You do not get to talk to me like a mother. You are not my mother. You're a member of the Universal Council. So, Council Member Griffith, what will you do with the horrible person who tried to save Queen Sindra, her friend, from death? How will you punish the woman who would have saved hundreds of fairies from the same fate? *Surely*, I deserve nothing less than annihilation."

Shirley the pixie popped up in front of me, her dirt-brown wings beating the air angrily behind her. She crossed her pudgy arms, opened her lips to yell at me, and then seemed to realize where she was and squeaked, popping away in another burst of light.

The twelve members of the council all spoke at once. It had been them I'd heard arguing, I realized, as Maddie had shifted me there.

"The Council cannot offer special favors for one species. If we do, we'll soon be overrun with requests," said a small, blocky man with a piglike nose and horns curving around his pointed ears.

"Sindra is a good queen. She deserves special consideration..." said a woman next to my mother whose features reminded me of a fish. There was something flopping around beneath the dais that looked like a giant fin.

"She is no more or less special than anyone else," said a pinch-faced man with slicked-back black hair and oversized canines. A vampire? Ugh.

A creature with silky brown hair covering every visible inch of his tree-like body swayed toward the vampire. His voice was deep and slow, exhibiting a calmness that slowed the rapid beat of my heart. "All creatures deserve special consideration, councilman. Even your reprehensible kind."

Explosions of outrage followed the tree man's comment,

precipitating a pounding of the gavel in the leader's hand. "Silence!"

The room fell quiet. The councilman in the center of the platform looked at Madeline. "PTB Quilleran, do you have any insights into this problem?"

She stepped forward, and when she did, the haziness of my surroundings slid away and I gasped. There was nothing beneath or around us except for blue sky and clouds. It was as if we were hanging in the sky without anything to hold us up.

I panicked, my hands flying out and my knees bending as if I could jump to a firm spot. Dizziness swamped me, I swayed, black dots filling my sight, and I thought I would pass out. A warm hand found my arm. The gentle but firm grip somehow eased the dizziness away. I turned to look into my mother's eyes.

Damp eyes, filled with tears. "I'm sorry," she whispered for my ears only. "I promise, I'll explain."

"Council Griffith?" the bulgy-eyed leader queried.

She nodded. "We're good here. The girl just became dizzy for a moment."

To my surprise, his lips curved into a pleasant smile. "It is a slightly disconcerting thing, hanging in the sky. I understand."

I bit back a snotty response and realized I'd definitely been hanging around with Sebille for too long.

"As you were saying?" the leader urged Maddie.

The witch favored me with a commiserating glance and then said, "My brother has given the Keeper one hour to find the fairies or give him the key. After that, he assures me they will all die."

I felt faint again. But not because of the no floor, no walls thing. It was from hearing that we had so little time. And the stupid Council had just made sure we'd lost precious moments of that limited timeframe.

No doubt seeing me stiffen with anger, my mother gave my arm a warning squeeze. "I'll deal with this," she promised softly. Then, lifting her head and her voice, she called for a special time dispensation. "I request we turn back the clock to the moment Jacob Quilleran disappeared. Under the circumstances, it is fitting that we give my daughter and her friends the time to find the fairies without council interference or any show of preference. Our involvement needn't be an issue. It is just a KoA and her friends trying to save a valued member of the magical universe." She sent a scathing glance toward the vampire on the council. "Despite what Marcus believes, Queen Sindra *is* important to our world and deserves saving."

The council thought about that for a moment and then the leader glanced down the dais in both directions. Every head except the vampire's nodded in agreement. Then, with a final pound of his gavel, the agreement was made. "It is done."

Madeline reached for me and, in the blink of an eye, the world fell away again.

22

TOADSTOOL CITY!

Croakies was in an uproar. Sebille had called Rustin and Lea back and they were yelling at each other, trying to figure out where Madeline had taken me. Archie seemed to be in the middle of things, looking perplexed.

Madeline dropped me amid the stacks and touched my shoulder, whispering. "Good luck Naida keeper." And then she was gone, goddess-be-danged! I knew why she wasn't helping. Her help would be seen by others as interference by the Council.

Still.

I frowned at the spot where she'd been, wishing politics didn't always have to be such a big part of my world.

"I assure you, if I knew why she'd been taken I'd tell you. As it is, I've been so caught up in trying to find the fairies, I don't even know what day or hour it is." Archie scrubbed a hand over his bristly cheeks, his color still not good.

"This is clearly because we stole the key. They're going to lock her up," Rustin said. He sounded sincerely worried, his voice vibrating slightly as if he were pacing. "Did you ask the cop?" he barked at someone.

Sebille expelled an angry breath. "I have a call into him but he's not calling me back."

"Grym's probably trying to find out what happened before he calls," Lea suggested.

I stepped out from between the book shelves. "Hey," I said. Every head whipped my way. Lea hurried over to hug me and Archie sagged in relief.

"We were so worried. What happened?" my bestie asked.

"Miss!" Hobs threw himself into my arms and squeezed me tight. Wicked wound around my ankles, his tail snapping.

"Thank the goddess," Baca said from somewhere above my head.

I looked up to find her perched atop the front row of shelves. It was her and Hobs' favorite spot. The little brownie gave me a shy smile.

I set Hobs back onto his feet and scooped up Wicked, burying my face in his sweet-smelling fur. "I have quite the story for you all. But we don't have time for it right now. Jacob told Madeline we have one hour to find the fairies or give him the key."

Sebille's eyes widened. "Do you still have it? The key?"

I shook my head, frowning. "The Council has it. Another long story." I glanced at my uncle. "Anything?"

He nodded. "We've managed to isolate the fairies' magical signature to somewhere in the Enchanted Forest."

I held back a groan, but just barely. The forest had nearly endless acreage, filled with lots of deadly things. There were no hard and fast rules in the forest. Nothing worked as expected. Even the locations of specific objects or places shifted at the whim of a magic user. Finding the fairies there, especially within an hour, would be a nearly impossible task.

I didn't look at Archie, not wanting him to see my disappointment. The silence permeating the room told me I wasn't the only one who knew how bad the odds were against us.

"I know it's not much," Archie said, his tone soothing. "But it's not as bad as it sounds. I have magic readers monitoring the forest for any signs of Jacob Quilleran. We're also looking for Sindra's signature. My guess is he's got them locked into a rogue void. After our adventure with the Altas Magnanimus, I have sensors all over that forest looking for abnormal void activity. We'll find them, Naida girl."

I fought the words wanting to spill from my lips, but Sebille said them for me. "Not in less than an hour." She dropped to a chair, every line of her skinny form rounded with defeat.

I fought my own feelings of loss, unwilling to give up with time still on the clock. "How close can you get us to the spot where their signature was found?" I asked Archie.

He frowned thoughtfully. "The signal weakens after five miles. So, a circular space of five miles is our search area."

I nodded, grabbing my purse from a cabinet in the tea area. "Let's go," I told my friends.

Sebille's head slowly lifted. "Where?"

"To find your mother."

"There isn't time."

Anger slid in to replace the despair. It wasn't like her to give up. "Yes. There is. We'll spread out and search that five-mile-radius, using every last minute if we need to. I'm not giving up on them, Sebille. Are you?"

She stared at me for a long moment, her jaw tight and her jewel-like eyes hard with anger. I got it. I really did.

What had happened to her mother wasn't fair. Not even close. But we hadn't gone through everything we had just to give up because it got too hard.

Finally, her chin rose a fraction and I knew I had her. She stood. "Okay. Let's go."

My phone rang as we headed outside. I nearly ignored it, but realized it would be stupid to ignore what could possibly be help. When I glanced at the ID, I was glad I hadn't. "Grym, we're going to look for the fairies…"

"Good. Wait for me," he said, interrupting. "I'm on my way to you. We just got a report of unusual activity near the Phantom Ridge of Enchanted Mountain."

Phantom Ridge was called that because it was almost always bathed in a pale gray fog, day or night and year around. But something else niggled about the location. I just couldn't pinpoint what. "What kind of unusual activity?" I had no idea what could be construed as unusual magical activity in an enchanted forest. Everything was unusual there.

"Fire. But when the fire department went to check it out, they realized they weren't looking at normal flames. It's not burning anything or spreading. It's magical fire."

Hope sprang into my chest. "That is unusual."

Sebille grabbed my shoulder. "What's happening?"

"Grym says there's magical fire near Phantom Ridge."

"That's within our search radius," Archie said.

Sebille's eyes went round. "Are you thinking what I am?"

I probably wasn't, but seeing the connections click into place in her eyes, I remembered why I knew that place.

We both said it at the same time. "Toadstool City!"

∾

TOADSTOOL CITY HAD BEEN Queen Sindra's queendom and the home for all the fairies under her rule. Set in the middle of the forest, the place was magically hidden from non-magical humans, who were dissuaded from coming too close by wards and spells they didn't recognize as anything but a strange reluctance to travel in a certain direction.

The fairies had lived in the pretty little city for hundreds of years, happily beautifying and caring for their own little part of the world. They'd been an important part of the ecosystem, protected by their own magic and the animals of the natural world, which had instinctively understood their importance and value to the ecosystem.

We spread out and walked carefully through the forest, our eyes and ears peeled for any sign of Jacob or anything else that might try to stop us from saving the fairies.

Grym's guy in the fire department was standing by the site, watching to make sure nothing stumbled across the no longer warded site and damaged whatever was left of the place. The fairies had been forced to move out of Toadstool City after a fire Jacob Quilleran himself had orchestrated burned the fairies' home to the ground.

The thought still made me sad. And, though the event had brought the fairies into Lea's greenhouse and more intimately into our lives, I still regretted the loss the queen and her subjects had suffered. It had been devastating to them. I had a feeling it was that loss of control over their lives that was spurring Sindra to move to a new queendom in the Primordial Forest.

The greenhouse was not technically her queendom since it belonged to Lea. And Sindra had declared she'd never return to the Enchanted Forest. She said she'd never feel safe there again. But a hidden grotto deep in the Primordial Forest, where, as it happened, her other children currently made their home, understandably held some appeal to her.

I sighed, wishing we didn't have to say goodbye to the fairies whom I'd gotten close to and enjoyed so much. My understanding of their plight only made it harder, because I realized I didn't have a right to ask them to stay.

Shoving thoughts of my impending loss, whichever way the current problem turned out, I cast my senses out and immersed myself in the forest as we approached our destination.

The Enchanted Forest was dense with trees. Covered in rich hues of green, their arms reached high into a cloudless blue sky and rustled softly in a warm breeze. The trunks of the ancient trees were bigger around than I was, some of them twice my size. Wild flowers in all sizes, colors, and shapes dug their roots into the rich black soil around the massive trees' far-flung feet.

The wonderful mix of smells ran the gamut from the earthiness of the fertile soil to the variety of natural floral perfumes painting the breeze.

The forest was far from quiet. Its music encompassed a mix of nature's songs, from the belching of fat bullfrogs along the wide creek to the happy chirp of a thousand busy insects. I missed the musical voices of the sprites, fairies, and elves that had once populated the mystical forest.

I soon spotted the flickering colors of living fire dancing between the trees not too far ahead. I braced for what I was going to find, fearing I'd be looking at a graveyard of charred plants and ashy ground. It had still been smoking when Sebille and I had found it after Jacob's desecration, and I'd never forget the feelings the sight had caused.

My mind cast back to the playful beauty that had once been Toadstool City and I wished it would live again. I stepped through the trees and, as if I'd pulled the city whole from my imagination, it was there again in front of me.

A perfect replica of Queen Sindra's former queendom.

Stretched out beneath the protective arms of what I'd always thought was the forest's largest tree, with the clear sparkling water of Magic Creek as its southern boundary, were hundreds of toadstools, nestled close and filling every inch of available space.

They were all different sizes and shapes, colors and patterns. The mix included pretty green toadstools covered in delicate brown spots, oversized white ones with tawny underbellies, even tree-shaped toadstools whose surface reminded me of brains. There were pink ones with purple stripes, yellow ones with orange spots, and stools with lacy underbellies that looked like old-fashioned petticoats. Dispersed strategically among the rest, were toadstools that were so vibrantly blue they mirrored the hues of the sky above. Sebille had once explained that those particular stools were warded to give warnings on a variety of things, from dangerous weather, to approaching airborne preda-tors, or inadvertent intruders of the human or supernormal variety.

Sebille and Lea stepped through the trees behind me and gasped. We stood there staring at the impossible for several beats, the sprite's fingers clutching my arm like talons.

As the shock wore off, the pain from her nails digging into me finally seeped in and I reached over to loosen her hand, stepping away from it. "Do you have a chip?"

Sebille's gaze widened. She gave me a look that told me she only half believed what we were seeing was real.

Chips were like keys that had given access to the city for non-resident fae and visiting dignitaries.

Sebille chewed her lip as she returned her attention to the city which was, literally, under fire. The flames seemed to sit atop the city, but weren't burning it or spreading.

"It's back?" Rustin asked, taking it much better than we had. He wandered closer, squatting down beside the toadstools and eyeing the magical flames. He glanced back at Sebille. "Did your mother know?"

The sprite shrugged, her face chalky, as if she were looking at a ghost.

In a way, I guessed she was.

Grym pushed past us and went to talk to his guy. I watched as a man stepped from the trees, no doubt keeping his distance from the fire so he could observe without being observed himself.

Brad Spence was about five feet eleven with golden-brown eyes and fiery red hair that rivaled Sebille's for brightness. He was also a phoenix shifter, which made him a perfect fireman.

The two men spoke for a minute and then came over to the rest of us. Brad nodded at Lea and Sebille and then fixed his gaze on me. "Naida keeper."

I smiled. "Hey, Brad." I genuinely liked the soft-spoken man, and he *had* saved my life from a wizard once. I'd never be able to repay him for that.

"Brad says nobody's come near the fire since he got here. But he says there's been some magical activity from Toadstool City."

That drew Lea's gaze from the fire. "What kind of magical activity?" she asked.

Brad shrugged. "Random flares. A couple of times a pale green mist sifted up through the fire. I thought it was going to put the fire out for a minute, but it didn't quite manage that."

"Any sign of the fairies?" Archie asked the fireman.

"No fairies."

We all deflated a little.

"But there's been a really big owl sitting up in that tree a couple of times. I think it's gone off to hunt now. But it might come back."

Grym, Lea, Sebille, and I shared a look.

An owl.

Margot Quilleran had presented herself as an owl. She was currently rotting in prison, but maybe shifting into an owl was a Quilleran trick? I turned to find Rustin heading back our way. "Can your uncle shift into a great owl?"

Rustin frowned. "Yeah. The whole family could. I might even still be able to. It's part of our magic legacy."

The news made my chest hurt. Sebille clenched her fists, and Lea kicked angrily at a stone near her shoe. I glanced at my cell for the time. We had fifteen minutes before Jacob swooped back down and destroyed our lives.

Grym looked up into the huge tree that protected Toadstool City from harsh weather.

Brad was right. There was currently no owl in the tree. But that didn't mean he wasn't nearby.

"This Jacob is the one who took the fairies?" Brad asked.

"Yeah," Grym said. "And I'm betting that fire is keeping them locked in there until he decides what to do with them."

"Not for long," I said. "We're getting them out of there." I looked at Sebille. "A chip?"

She nodded and walked over to the trunk of the protective tree, circling it until she disappeared. She returned a minute later with a small stone, brushing soil off its surface with a finger.

I arched a brow at her.

"What?"

"Are you seriously telling me you did the equivalent of a key under the mat for your mother's queendom?"

She shrugged. "I kept forgetting to bring a chip."

I rolled my eyes so hard I could see Grym's wry smile behind me. Okay, not really, but work with me here.

Hoo hoo hoo hoo hu hu.

I jumped as the hooting owl call filled the dusky air, followed by a second call in the distance.

Hoo hoo hoo hoo hu hu.

"Please tell me there aren't two of them."

"Let's hope not," Grym said. "But we'd better get moving, just in case."

I glanced around, looking for Archie. He'd wandered away from the burning city shortly after we'd arrived, looking for something. I figured he was still working under the void theory. "Archie?" I called softly, not wanting to alert Jacob if he was nearby.

Hoo hoo hoo hoo hu hu.

My pulse spiked.

"We need to get inside," Sebille said. "We're running out of time."

"I know. But I want Archie with us."

"Why?" Grym asked. "I was going to go."

"If this Quilleran guy is coming back," Brad said. "I'm going to need you out here to help me fight him off."

I nodded. "If we get into trouble once inside the city, Archie can pull us all into a void and keep us safe until Jacob's either gone or caught."

I knew by the look on Grym's face that my idea made sense. Though he wasn't happy about splitting up.

"I can help with my uncle," Rustin said.

"I'm coming with you," Lea said to me. "If there's a way

to magic them out of there, maybe Sebille and I can manage it together."

Not for the first time, I regretted my worthless defensive capabilities. "Okay, let's do this."

A large shadow painted the ground around us, and I glanced up to find the biggest owl I'd ever seen swooping down on us from the sky. The bird's oversized eyes looked way too human for my comfort, and its razor-sharp talons reached for us as if we were mice. "Watch out!"

23

FOLLOW ME AS SOON AS YOU CAN!

A large body slammed into me, driving me to the ground. Grym's big hand cupped my face to keep it from smashing into the ground, and he held his weight off me as we landed. Lea screamed and my head came up as Grym pushed off the ground. "Get to cover!" he yelled, launching himself toward the spot where the owl was attacking Lea and Sebille. To her credit, the sprite was holding her ground. She was firing magic at the big predator even as she dodged the slicing force of his talons. Unfortunately, the powerful magic simply bounced off the air around the owl, proving, if we'd had any doubts, that we weren't dealing with a natural owl.

I scrambled toward a large bush as a bright light flashed, leaving Grym standing in his gargoyle form. He reached up and grasped one leg of the monstrous bird, yanking it away from Sebille as it slashed at her with its talons.

"Lea!" I called, motioning her toward the bush where I hid.

Sebille glanced our way and then turned and ran in the opposite direction, toward the massive tree protecting Toadstool City. She slammed her palm into the tree and a flare of green magic shot out from around her hand before easing away. Sebille's long, skinny body shrank to sprite form and she flew in our direction, dodging around the battle a few feet away. Something dropped from her tiny fist, hitting the ground near my feet. "I'm going in," she said. "Follow me as soon as you can."

"No, Sebille!" But the sprite wasn't waiting. I couldn't really blame her. We were seriously running out of time.

"Wait," Lea said. "How are we going to get inside? Didn't she just use up the only chip?"

I shook my head, reaching for the small rock by my feet. "She doesn't need it to get inside. She engaged it for us. We just need to get within a few inches of the tree and we'll be sucked inside."

Lea nodded as a roar filled the area. Rustin shifted to his chimera, bright light illuminating the world around us with a strange, yellow glow.

Jacob's owl slashed at Grym, scoring a strike across his chest and earning himself freedom from the gargoyle's grip on his leg. The owl soared into the sky and, for a moment, I thought Jacob was running. But the owl didn't fly away. He flew in a tight circle and dropped his talons into hunting mode again. Wings up, Jacob dropped onto Rustin's back.

The chimera roared, fire bathing the clearing, and Grym had to jump out of the way to keep from being singed.

The owl ripped at Rustin's furry back with its talons and pecked violently at his head and face with its curved beak.

"We need to go," I said, pushing Lea toward the tree.

She held back. "We should help," she said in a worried voice. "Rustin's getting really hurt."

I glanced at the chimera in time to see him drop to the ground and roll, trying to smash the owl beneath him.

"No, he's okay. Look."

Brad joined the battle, a long blade in each hand, slashing at the owl as Rustin climbed back to his feet.

Grym ran over and grabbed at the flailing owl, trying to get his big hands around its neck.

I averted my eyes, not wanting to see Jacob's owl get decapitated. "Hurry, Lea." I glanced at my phone. "We have six minutes to get the fairies out." I gave Lea a little push and we took off running. Halfway there, another roar filled the night. I couldn't help it, I looked that way, and what I saw had my heart stuttering painfully in my chest.

Brad was down, bleeding from deep talon marks across his middle, and it didn't look like he was getting up anytime soon. He was out cold.

The owl had managed to escape Grym and Rustin, and was hovering just above the ground. With a strident cry, it began to stretch, elongate, and then, in a rush of caustic magic that flung Grym to the ground and had Rustin turning his massive lion face away, the owl turned into something else.

Something that turned my blood to ice.

The enormous snake that was Jacob Quilleran hit the ground with a meaty sound and immediately lashed out, barely missing Grym's arm with what looked like five-inch-long fangs.

Rustin lunged, and the snake whipped its thick tail in his direction, curling around his back leg so fast I thought I was seeing things.

Rustin went down with a roar and Grym leaped at the snake.

Quick as a wink, the thirty-foot-long python with saber fangs and a spiky ridge of black and cream speckled feathers ridging its back, sank its teeth into Grym's muscular leg.

The gargoyle threw back his head and bellowed.

The giant snake flung its head and yanked Grym to the ground, pulling him toward its huge maw.

Without thinking, I started to run toward Grym.

An arm snagged me around the waist and yanked me back. "No, Naida," my uncle hissed. "Let them manage Quilleran. We must save the fairies."

I knew Archie was right. But the thought of leaving Grym behind when it looked as if he was about to be swallowed whole by that...thing.

I couldn't do it.

"Let me go!" I screamed. I fought Archie every step of the way, arms and legs flailing in an attempt to get to Grym. But my strength was no match for his.

A moment later, as Grym was pulled mere inches from the reptile's terrible jaws, I felt the fairy magic grab me. Panic clawed through my chest, drawing a desperate scream from my lips. "Grym!" I shrieked. The magic burned as it slid over me, starting at my toes and rising quickly up my legs, torso, hands, arms, neck, and then my head.

A deep, red flush followed the magic over my body, until all visible skin was the color of an overripe tomato. The burn increased, causing me to grit my teeth against the pain. I ground down on my desire to return to Grym. If I fought the magic and rejected it, our chip would be rendered null and void. And the fairies would lose their chance to survive.

Tears burned my eyes as my feet touched down in what to all intents and purposes was fairy.

Flower-scented air whispered over me and I opened my eyes. Unlike the last time I'd visited Toadstool City, the chip had drawn us directly through the gates into the city. It must have had something to do with Sebille engaging it for us.

A beat later, the earth rumbled and shook beneath our feet and, for the briefest moment, I thought Jacob's trap was already springing.

But then a massive snake tail slammed into the space before the fairy gate and I sighed in relief that Sebille had greased the path for us. If we'd shrunk to fairy size and walked through the gates as was usual, we'd likely have been killed or blocked by that goddess-be-danged snake.

"Three minutes," Archie bellowed as he started running down the street toward the largest structure at the end.

"How do we know where to look for them?" Lea asked, her words breathless from running.

I shook my head. "We don't. But, they're clearly not in the streets. The palace is the only place big enough to hold them all. It's a calculated guess."

Lea nodded and we fell silent as we ran.

The toadstools that framed the web of narrow streets appeared to be the size of human buildings from our diminutive perspective. Normally they would be filled with hundreds of walking, flying, and gliding Fae. But they were empty. Silent.

The first glimmer of fear that we'd been too late tightened my belly and sent prickles along my arms.

I looked up at the sky. It was a dark lilac as the sun evacuated its spot to make room for the moon to play. Normally, when night fell in Toadstool City, it went into lockdown. Magical aversion warding worked in tandem with protective spider webbing to keep everyone who lived in the city safely inside the gates. It also kept those who didn't belong firmly outside the protections.

I doubted the warding was in place, given that the entire

city was probably just a contrived glamour courtesy of Jacob Quilleran. But if he'd kept to the spirit of the magic, we'd be locked into Toadstool City for the night. I had no idea how that would fit into Jacob's diabolical trap, but I guessed it was too late to worry about.

Queen Sindra's palace was located in the center of Toadstool City. All roads led to the palace, and it rose above the other structures both in size and vitality of color. With a massive, domed roof painted a vibrant purple and covered with bright yellow splotches, the palace formed the perfect center point, the city's roads a lively array of toadstool-lined spokes radiating from it.

As we hurried down the too-empty street toward the palace, I began to dread what we'd find there. An acidic nub of worry had burrowed into my belly, and I couldn't shake the surety that we'd be too late.

We ran up the wide, mossy steps to the rounded yellow door of the entrance. Normally, two elves dressed in the solid black attire of the queen's guards would block our entry and demand to hear our business with the queen. Though the process was intimidating, I suddenly wished to see those elves, and the business-as-usual process of the fairies' everyday lives.

The haunting silence of the city was getting to me. The possibility that we'd been too late was making my steps heavy.

Archie looked at the entry room, which was octagonal, with doors branching off in eight directions. He looked at me. "Naida? Do you know the way to the queen's chambers?"

I nodded and plunged through a door, moving quickly and from memory. Unfortunately, I'd only been there twice and the palace was built like a honeycomb, consisting of hundreds of small, octagonally-shaped rooms that served as buffers and barriers to the central space where the queen held court. I took the wrong door more than once, before finally stumbling out of a room and into the central hive area.

We stepped into a large room with a high ceiling. The remembered scent hit me first. The entire perimeter of the octagonal space was lined with layers of flowering plants and trees. It smelled fresh and sweet, like growing things, and nostalgia hit me hard between the eyes.

There was no constant buzzing of wings filling the space. No bees bustling from bloom to bloom as if they were driven by a single purpose.

No Sindra flying from hive to hive, inspecting and correcting her workers.

No movement at all, except for the slender sprite kneeling over her mother's too-still form, quaking with sobs.

24

PLAN B RIDES AGAIN

"I guess Jacob lied to us about turning the fairies into motes," I murmured to Lea.

"Shocking," my friend said, shaking her head. "What an evil derf he is."

"We have less than two minutes," Archie said quietly.

I started to run, stepping carefully through the bodies of the fairies, who'd been laid out around the queen. Sindra had been painstakingly arranged with her wings outspread and her hands crossed over her belly. Her gown shimmered with magical light through the dimness of the room, all other light having been sucked out of the place, as it had the inhabitants.

I dropped to my knees next to Sebille. "Is she...?"

Sebille lifted an angry, tear-stained visage to me. "He'll pay for this."

My own tears answered hers. "She's not...?"

Sebille shook her head, sniffling. "She's alive. But they all seem to be in some state of suspended animation. I've tried everything to wake them up. Nothing's worked."

Relief filled me. "One step at a time. Let's work on

getting them to safety. The rest will work itself out." They were brave words, but I couldn't help scanning the room and all the bodies. We couldn't possibly move them all in...

"One minute," Archie said, joining us near the queen.

Sebille glowered up at him, before turning back to me. "We have no time."

"Stop bawling like a baby," Lea barked from behind Archie. "We didn't come all this way just to stand here and watch them die."

She was right. I pulled out the Book of Pages. "We need all of them touching hands," I told Sebille and Lea. "Hurry."

We jumped to our work, running around the room connecting as many fairies as we could for the transfer.

I had no idea if we could even move so many bodies through the book. But I was hoping their relative size would work in our favor.

And we really had no choice but to try.

I realized after a moment that Archie wasn't helping. "Archie!" I yelled.

He flipped a hand in my direction. "I'm working on Plan B."

Shaking my head, I stepped up my pace. "How much time?"

"Thirty seconds," Sebille screamed.

I moved faster, occasionally tripping over a slender arm or leg and yelling an apology into the ether.

"Twenty seconds," Sebille yelled, her tone slightly hysterical.

I glanced at my uncle, finding him talking to himself, his fingers forming shimmering silver mathematical equations on the air.

"Ten seconds," Sebille shrieked.

"We need to go," I yelled, running to the book.

"But there are more!" Lea cried out.

I motioned for her to come. "You two take the ones we've connected. Archie and I will bring the last of them."

I had no idea if that was true, but I handed Sebille the book. As co-manager of the artifact library, Sebille could work the book as well as I could.

"Five seconds," Archie yelled.

I grabbed Lea's hand and looked Sebille in the eyes. "You can do this."

I didn't wait for their response. I started running, not wanting to get caught up in the whirlwind once the book started gathering up its travelers.

The magic hissed and there was a long, low groan of energy as I reached Archie. "We're out of time, Uncle. Bring on Plan B."

All the air in the room seemed to suck inward, tugging me and Archie with it for a beat before it coalesced into a whirlwind over the book and then sucked everyone through with a drawn-out hiss of displaced air.

And then they were gone.

All except for about a dozen fairies on the outer layers we hadn't been able to connect.

The floor beneath our feet rumbled. The structure groaned.

Light flared beyond the glass roof above, a sickly yellow illumination that painted the entire city in a putrid glow.

Magic chewed on my skin. Ugly, dark magic. I knew without asking my uncle that it hadn't come from him.

Jacob had engaged his malicious plan. We were about to die.

A strange calm slipped over me. My friends were safe. Goddess-willing, Grym and Rustin were still alive. We'd managed to save the queen and most of her court.

It wasn't perfect. I thought of the dozen fae who hadn't made the rescue. Tears burned my eyes. Queen Sindra, Lea, and Sebille would mourn their loss.

They'd also mourn mine, and Archie's. They'd be sad. But they'd be alive.

We'd kept Jacob from doing his worst. We'd survived Mission Implausible and hadn't been thrown into Casa De Grimoire. And, I'd lived a good life. Not a long one, but a good one. An exciting one. I'd made friends, found family, had successes and failures. I thought of Wicked, Hobs, Vel, and Slimy and the tears fell more freely.

"Barking banshee bunions, Naida!" Archie screamed at me. "A little help here?"

I blinked, coming back to reality.

"Huh?" I looked over at Archie, who appeared to be holding the slit in a massive void open, the wind blowing his robes around his skinny legs and his expression dark with strain. I glanced around, finding the floor empty. The remaining fairies were gone!

"How'd you get them all inside?" I ran toward him, ducking through the slit just as the room outside exploded into a billion shiny points of light.

Archie released the opening and it snapped shut, enclosing us in unbreakable, velvet darkness. "I created a void pull. Easy really."

I laughed. Yeah. Easy.

There were a few tense beats of silence as we waited to see if we'd go up in flames with Toadstool City. The silence extended after the tension eased, only the sound of our breathing filling the unnatural quiet.

Then Archie cleared his throat. "What in the twelve dimensions were you doing out there? It looked like you were performing a Shakespearean soliloquy or something."

I felt my lips tip upward. A wide smile slowly broke free. And then I was laughing so hard my knees gave out beneath me and I dropped to the spongy floor of Archie's void, falling to my back and scraping tears from my cheeks. I lay there for a minute, catching my breath.

Archie eased down beside me, sighing.

"This is a really good void," I told my uncle, reaching through the darkness for his hand. His fingers clasped mine and squeezed.

"It is, isn't it," he said. And then we were laughing again, the sound the freest expression of relief we could find.

I WAS DREAMING ABOUT BUTTERFLIES. Lots of butterflies. Really big butterflies. Butterflies chasing me and whacking me on the face with their wings.

The dream should have awoken me, but it took a certain deep voice calling my name to finally break through my exhaustion and drag me from sleep.

I opened my eyes to impenetrable darkness, and immediately thought I was still dreaming and my eyes were still closed.

Then Archie's voice reminded me where we were. "Did you hear that?" His voice was rusty, as if he'd been ripped from sleep like I'd been.

"Somebody's calling for Naida," a male voice said from just behind me.

I jumped, yelping, and blinked rapidly as a ball of light burst into existence, illuminating an array of elves, pixies, and sprites.

"You're awake!" I exclaimed, excited.

Several judgmental adolescent faces looked back at me.

A young sprite, probably a teen judging from his clothes and mannerisms, snorted a laugh. "Says the one who slept the longest of all of us."

Several titters joined his laughter and I looked around, realizing we had a group of teen fae in the void with us.

"I'm starving, man," a spiky-haired youth said. "You got any junk food?"

I laughed in delight. "Nope. No food."

"You don't have to be so happy about it," said a cute young pixie from the back. She tossed her blonde bob and rolled her eyes exuberantly. "Humans are weird." She emphasized the proclamation with a flutter of her drab, brown wings.

They skimmed across my cheek and I realized the source of my butterfly dreams.

I laughed again. "We are, aren't we?"

They all looked at me like I'd lost my mind. There was a really good chance I had. Then I remembered something I needed to worry about. "We have to get out of here. I need to know if Grym and Rustin are all right. And the others. What if they didn't make it back to the library? What if they got lost in the ether or something?"

Archie flashed a look at the kids. "Ixnay on the ostlay in the etheray," he murmured.

"Oh yeah, man. Like we don't know iglattenplay. We're not iveflay, you know," said the teen, whose black hair and silver wings told me he was an elf.

The other kids laughed uproariously at this.

I grabbed Archie's arm. "Get us out of here, okay?"

He shook his head. "I think we should stay a while longer. We don't know what Quilleran did to the city? There might be toxic air..."

Naida!

I jumped, recognizing that distant, worried voice. "It's Grym!" I reached out until my hand touched the side of the void and started to pound. "I'm here! We're all here, Grym."

Archie grabbed my arm and gently shoved me to the side. "If they're walking around out there, it's okay to leave."

"Inallyfay," said the wiseacre kid. "I'm arvingstay."

I glanced at the young elf as Archie worked on opening the void. "You aren't by any chance related to Sebille, are you?"

The kids laughed. The wiseacre shook his head. "No. But she's my hero," he said with a grin.

"Of course she is."

25

AM I GOING TO HAVE TO ARREST YOU?

It turned out that we'd been stuck in Archie's little void for twenty-four hours. Archie kept insisting that we weren't gone that long according to his moon-watch. But he admitted the fact that we were basically in an alien dimension, a.k.a. an unknown void, might have skewed the watch's internal calculations.

For my part, I was just hoping twenty-four hours without eating might have actually carved a few pounds off of me. Alas, when I stepped on the scale in my apartment, it appeared I'd *gained* two pounds.

The Universe was clearly punishing me.

So, with nothing to lose...literally...I decided tacos would be a good idea for dinner. Fortunately, Grym was on his way over anyway, so I asked him to pick up our order for us.

Sebille was making tea and Rustin was regaling us with stories about how he and Grym had defeated Jacob Quilleran in all his forms. Apparently, the powerful witch had also been able to transform into a super-sized weasel when appropriately inspired. No surprise there.

Fortunately for everyone, the witch was on his way to

Casa De Grimoire. As a sorcerer in good standing at the Société of Dire Magic, and since he'd had a hand in capturing Jacob...sort of...Archie was accompanying Grym and Brad Spence as they transported Jacob to the super-max facility.

He was very excited.

Sebille gave Rustin and me our tea and sat down with us at the table. She looked happier than I'd seen her in a while and it made me want to smile. When she made fun of me for my "goofy" grin. I just grinned wider. "So, what really happened to the fairies?" I asked the sprite. I still hadn't gotten the full story of the fake Toadstool City and how the fae had ended up there.

Sebille sipped her tea, taking her time.

I rolled my eyes and sighed.

Finally, she set her cup down. "As we've already figured out, Jacob did lie about turning them into dust. His magic that day ripped them out of the greenhouse and dumped them into the glamour he'd created of Toadstool City. Mother verified that they were in some type of suspended animation the whole time."

Rustin frowned. "Brad said he saw magic coming out of there."

Sebille nodded. "Mother was immobile, but she was able to create some magic with her mind. She actually created those flames, hoping someone would see them and report it to fire and police."

"Smart," I said, sipping my tea.

Sebille nodded. "What Brad saw was her making sure the magic stayed active." The sprite frowned. "She admitted she was about at the end of her energy though. If we hadn't found her when we did..." She frowned.

I patted her arm. "Stop that. We did find them. And everybody's okay."

Sebille nodded. "Oh, and mother said when she appeared to us here, she wasn't saying we should help Jacob. She was saying *don't* help him."

"Really?" I thought about what I'd seen and realized she could have been saying that. "I totally misread it."

The sprite shrugged.

"Is Lea coming over later?" I asked. I hadn't spoken much to my friend the witch since returning home. She'd been busily reconstructing her greenhouse with the help of Sindra and the fairies. Sebille had also been spending a lot of time out there, no doubt hoping to convince the queen to stay in Enchanted with us.

The success of her campaign was still unclear. Although, Lea had made the queen an offer she might not be able to refuse. Lea had offered to sell the structure to the fairies, the purchase of which would be financed in trade. The fairies would promise to grow herbs and other selected items for Lea's exclusive use for fifty years to work off the cost of the building.

There had even been some conversation about expanding the greenhouse to encompass the lot behind Croakies. An idea that I wholeheartedly supported.

Lea had assured the queen the contract could be broken at a future date if Sindra felt she needed to take her queendom elsewhere.

Between Lea's offer and Sebille's hard sell, we were hopeful the fairies would stay in Enchanted.

The front door opened and my head snapped up, my belly grumbling in anticipation of those tacos. Oh, and I was also excited to see Grym of course.

Heh.

But it wasn't Grym. And the woman who entered, her gaze sliding unerringly to mine, hadn't brought dinner.

Which was okay, because I'd suddenly lost my appetite. "Why are you here?"

Narina Griffith slid an intense hazel gaze over me and smiled. "Hello, Naida."

I lifted my brows and stared at her, unwilling to indulge in pleasantries.

Rustin and Sebille got up and went into the tea area, giving us at least the pretense of privacy.

My mother sighed, tucking her shoulder-length straight blonde hair behind a delicate ear. I'd gotten my height from her, but it seemed I hadn't inherited anything else. My own hair was dark brown from my dad's side, slightly curly, and tending to frizzy if I wasn't diligent with styling, which I rarely was. And, though we were both around five feet nine inches tall, my mother's build was slender and delicate, while I was...I'm gonna say big boned.

"I know you're annoyed with me..." she began.

"Hurt," I interrupted. I didn't want her using weasel words to relieve some of her guilt. If she even had guilt. "Suffering from feelings of abandonment. Perplexed. Feeling unloved." I cocked my head, frowning. "Take your pick. They all work."

Narina's hands twined in front of her. "The reasons we did what we did were good ones," she said. Then, seeing me stiffen with anger, she sighed again, shaking her head. "But looking back, I believe we were wrong."

I blinked in surprise. "Oh?"

She moved away from the door. "May I sit with you? Please?"

I hesitated a beat and then nodded. If I was going to be mad at her for doing what she did twenty-some years earlier, then I should at least know exactly what she did and her reasons for it.

Sebille returned to the table a minute later and handed Narina a steaming cup of tea.

"Ah, lovely. Thank you, dear."

Sebille gave me a wide-eyed look as my mother glanced away to sip her tea. My expression sent her a return message.

Sebille's look: Oh, my goddess!

My silent response: I know, right?

"I'm going to bed," Sebille said. "It's been a long day."

"Night," I said, wishing I could go to bed too.

"You look tired," Narina said.

"I am. We just got home a few hours ago."

Nodding, she said, "That was nicely done, by the way."

I fought the warmth blossoming in my chest at her compliment. "Which part, breaking into the vault? Or saving the fairies?"

Narina's laugh was light, infective. I had to fight my own smile. "Gunther was beside himself when you got past all his challenges." She shook her head. "He's going to be insufferable for months, until he comes up with new security challenges."

"Gunther?"

"Yes. Head Council. The man with the gavel."

I nodded, taking a sip of my lukewarm tea to gather my thoughts. I thought of all the questions I'd had for her over the years. Then decided to go for the most important one. "Tell me why you abandoned me."

She winced at the word. "We hadn't meant to. At the time, we thought it best to leave you with Neely."

I'd known her as Grandma Neely growing up. A troll, I'd later found out, and not my real grandmother, but rather my mother's old nanny. Neely had been a cold creature. I'd had very little in the way of affection growing up. Though I couldn't fault her care.

"There was this demi-god..." Narina rubbed her shoulders as if chilled by the memory. "He'd set his sights on getting the head spot on the Council and he saw me and your father as his main adversaries. After your father was killed..." Her face paled, as if she were reliving the horror of that time. She shook her head. "We later discovered Altham had killed him. He went after me next."

"Why didn't the Council do something?" I asked. "Surel..." I slapped my lips together, not wanting to summon the demon-pixie. "I mean, as one of the Council, it seems a no brainer that you'd be protected."

"They tried. But Altham was very powerful. No one could pin anything on him. And then he let me know he was going after my children, hoping it would be enough to make me step down."

A fresh wave of anger slipped through me. "But it wasn't. You decided instead to just get rid of your children and keep the job. Oh wait, you didn't get rid of both of us, did you? Only me."

"That's not fair, Naida." Her voice rising for the first time, Narina's cheeks regained their color. "Eddie was older than you and already powerful. His magic is so unique, Altham and his minions were unable to get close to him. But you..." She sighed. "We didn't know if you'd even have magic when you grew up. You were a late bloomer, magically. And since you were helpless and I was a single parent, I did the only thing I could think of to protect you." Tears glistened in her eyes. "You have no idea how hard it was."

I believed her. And she was right. I couldn't even imagine how hard it would be to walk away from a young child. But, against my will, I was starting to see her point. "Why didn't Neely help me find my magic?"

"I asked her not to." Narina's eyes flashed as I reacted with anger. She held up a hand. "I always intended to come back to you well before you gained your full power. But Altham proved harder to capture than we'd hoped. And the years slipped by. Without Eddie and I there to protect you, it was dangerous for you to have magic."

"How did you finally catch him?" I asked, curious about the creature who'd cost me my family.

She sipped her tea, her motions slightly stiff and uncomfortable looking. And when she finally lifted her gaze to mine, I tensed. Her hazel gaze offered such depths of pain and regret. "You haven't found him yet, have you?"

Narina shook her head. She plucked at a stray thread on her pale-pink sweater, crossing her legs beneath her long, loose skirt. "As I said, he's proven to be more of a challenge than we'd expected."

I sat back in my chair, resignation and understanding finally hitting me. "That's why you and Eddie still don't come home."

She nodded. "Although you have your magic, it's not defensive. Which means you're still in danger if we acknowledge that you're family. Not to mention, my being on the Council. It makes you a target, Naida."

"Why don't you leave the Council?" I asked, not liking the slightly whiny tone in my voice.

"Altham's hatred of me has gone well beyond his desire for control of the Council, Naida. He only wants to punish me now. Harming you would be a perfect way to do that. Staying on the Council is the best way to protect you. The Council sees all that happens. We know what magics are being used and where. I know that demi-god's magic signature like I know my own. If he pops back up, I'll know where he is and I'm going to find him." Her eyes went hard at the declaration. "He won't threaten my family again and get away with it."

I believed her. My mother was a powerful wind sorceress. Eddie's chaos magic was terrifying. Between them...

I glanced at her. "Was Eddie with us on Nom so he could spy and report back to you?"

She actually chuckled, surprising me. "I wish I could claim that kind of power over him. But I'm afraid both of my children are stubborn and determined. Eddie didn't even warn me about what you were planning. He truly wanted to help, Naida. He's heartbroken that you're angry with him."

I wasn't sure if I could believe her, but I'd try to speak to my brother soon. If he really had tried to help, he deserved to at least tell me his side of things.

"Why did Uncle Archie suggest asking you to join us if he knew you were on the Council?" I asked.

She sighed. "Because he doesn't know. And, I'd appreciate it if you didn't tell him. The Council demands we keep our seats as hush-hush as possible. The secrecy protects everyone."

I nodded, then grinned. "Too bad. We really could have used you. Eddie was great, but he blew everything up a couple of times." I winced and she laughed.

"I still can't believe you got all the way to the key and out of the building with it." She reached out to tuck a strand of hair behind my ear, her expression filled with pride.

"It was just a copy," I told her, flushing with pleasure.

Narina nodded. "I'm aware. But even a copy of the rune key has the potential to create devastation in our world. It would have been very bad for Jacob Quilleran to get his hands on it."

I frowned, realizing we'd almost made a terrible mistake.

My mother's expression softened. "You are smart and determined, lovely Naida. I see a lot of your father in you." Her voice choked on her words and she cleared her throat, standing. "I'll let you get your rest. You and your friends have been given a special dispensation for your little field trip. But please, honey, don't do it again. I'm afraid my influence will only go so far in saving you."

I nodded, standing with her. I walked her to the door, feeling as if I was missing a chance to say something. Something important. When she stopped at the door and turned to me, I found myself in the position to remedy that. "Mom, I..."

Narina grabbed me and pulled me into a tight hug. "I love you too, lovely girl. And I promise that one day soon, we'll all be together again."

Tears leaked from my eyes as I nodded. "I'm going to hold you to that."

She pulled back and cupped my face with her hand. "Good. See you soon?"

"Let's do lunch. My people will call your people."

She laughed happily and walked out of Croakies, her step much lighter than it had been when she'd arrived.

I watched her walk down the street for a minute, not wanting to go back inside.

"Hey," Grym said, coming up the sidewalk a minute later with an enormous bag in one hand, and a giant-sized bakery box in the other. "Was that your mom leaving just now?"

I nodded.

"Am I going to have to arrest you?"

I laughed, snatching the bakery box from him. "Not before I've eaten, please."

He wrapped an arm around my waist and pulled me

close. "Have I told you that you scared the pebbles right out of me when you and Archie pulled that disappearing stunt?"

I leaned close, pressing my lips against his. The kiss started out with chaste intentions, but quickly grew heated as I found my happy place. My own, personal gargoyle was big and warm and strong and I relished every inch of him. When we broke the kiss a minute later, I sighed. "I have so much to tell you about my family and stuff."

He nodded. "You do. But let's eat first or I'll keep getting distracted by your grumbling stomach."

Laughing, I smacked him on the chest. "It's not nice to notice a lady's rumbling stomach."

"It's kind of hard to ignore." He set the bag of tacos on the table as the dividing door burst open. Hobs and Baca led the way, followed by Wicked and Hex. Wicked's sister was having a play date until Lea got done working in the greenhouse.

As if on cue, the front door opened and Lea came inside, looking tired and slightly disheveled, but happy. Rustin was on her heels. "I smell tacos," he announced.

"And donuts!" Lea added, diving into the box.

"Chocolate!" Hobs squealed, grabbing three chocolate glazed with his long fingers before I could stop him.

I looked at Grym and he grinned. "I have more food in the car. I know how things work in this place."

"I smell tacos," Sebille said from the dividing door. She was dressed in her red and white striped onesie pjs and her fire-engine red hair was loose, hanging past her waist. "I'm starving."

I was all but shoved away from the table as everybody moved in and grabbed food. I went to get napkins and paper plates, throwing them through the mass of bodies onto the table.

I laughed as they grabbed for the plates almost before they landed.

Grym came back inside with another big bag and another box. He held up the box. "Frosted brownies."

Hobs and Baca squealed and ran for the box, but Grym held it over his head. "For everybody," he warned on a chuckle.

"What's in the bag," I asked.

Behind him, the door opened again and Archie came inside. "What's for dinner, I'm starving." He saw the bag in Grym's outstretched hand and snagged it, looking inside. "Eggrolls!"

Even I squealed at that one.

A while later, my plate full of tacos, egg rolls, and more than one brownie, I leaned my head against Grym as lively conversation filled the room. I realized, finally, that I didn't need to feel badly about the family I'd lost all those years ago. I hadn't really lost them. And they were back in my life, despite their presence being spotty and less than normal.

More importantly, I'd built myself a new family. A happy and loving family who supported each other no matter what. And I realized in that moment that I was a very lucky girl.

Grym kissed my temple and wrapped a warm arm around my waist. I sighed happily.

Yep. A very lucky girl indeed.

The End

DON'T MISS OUT

Stay up on all Sam's news by joining her newsletter, and get a copy of a fun mystery just for signing up!

SIGN UP HERE!
https://samcheever.com/newsletter/

READ MORE ENCHANTING INQUIRIES

If you enjoyed **Croakies Dictum**, you might want to check out the rest of the series: https://samcheever.com/books/#enchanting

Enjoy this taste of Book 1: Unbaked Croakies:

~

How in the name of the goddess's favorite sports bra am I going to do this Magical Librarian job? I have no idea what I'm doing. And the woman who's supposed to be training me is...well, let's just say she's distracted and leave it at that. I guess I'll bumble through. It's become something of a trademark move for me.

My name is Naida Griffith and I'm a sorceress. I actually found that out not too long ago. I've lived with an undefined something burning in my belly for a while, feeling as if something wasn't quite right under my skin. Then, on my eighteenth birthday I started getting headaches. Bad ones. And random stuff started following me around.

Recently I was approached by a group called the Société of Dire Magic to become Keeper of the Artifacts. A magical librarian. Given that magical artifacts have taken to following me around, I decided I might have an aptitude for the job. So I said yes.

But in the first few days, I've been flogged by flip flops, bludgeoned by gnomes, and discovered a corpse in a suitcase. Then there's the woman who's supposed to be training me. She's...interesting.

Will I survive the training long enough to get the job as artifact librarian? You might as well ask me if a caterpillar gets manis or pedis. Who knows? But I know one thing for sure. This gig is hard.

I'm going to do my best to succeed. Or die trying.

UNBAKED CROAKIES

Oy, Pudsy. How's Things?

I stood on the street outside the bookstore, frowning up at the ugly wood sign with the picture of a spotted frog on it. The yellowed white paint was chipped and scarred, and there was a black blotch near the frog's mouth that looked like a fly.

I kept expecting the frog's tongue to snake out and snap it up.

It was an ugly sign. World-class ugly. But it was oddly suited given the store's strange name.

Croakies.

I mean. What kind of name was that for a bookstore?

Soft footsteps came up behind me and I resisted turning. "Are you ready?"

At just under six feet, the man was only a few inches taller than I was. I guessed he was about middle age. For a sorcerer that would put him in his eighties or nineties. He had piercing blue eyes that were a little darker than mine and longish, curly brown hair. He also had a truly forgettable face. I mean that literally. From one moment to the next I would often forget what the man looked like. In fact, the few times I'd seen him, I'd only been able to identify him because of the sorcerer's garb he wore.

The thought made me frown.

I always remembered the piercing blue gaze. And the hair. But that was all that stuck in my mind.

I knew him only as Agent A.P. from the Société of Dire Magic. A formidable group whose moniker seemed to strike fear into the hearts of everyone I spoke to about them. Supernormals, at least. Since I'd been raised by a non-magical grandma, I didn't really know that many supernormals. But the few I'd met since A.P. had knocked on my door a couple of weeks earlier, had seemed more than half afraid of him.

I had no idea what it was that scared them about the man. He seemed harmless enough to me.

I turned to look at the agent. He was less intimidating in his street clothes than he'd been in his robes. I'd only met him a handful of times. But each time we'd met previously, he'd looked just like a fairytale sorcerer in his long purple and black robes. All that had been missing was the pointy hat.

And the wand.

When I'd jokingly asked him where those two items were, he'd very earnestly explained that they were only for special ceremonies.

I hadn't known him long enough to recognize if he was joking.

I chose to believe he was.

Otherwise, it would just be too weird.

But back to his question. *Was I ready?*

Taking a deep, bracing breath, I nodded. I was as ready as I was ever going to be. With a feeling that my life was about to change in ways I couldn't imagine and might not like, I reached for the door to Croakies and opened it.

A mangy black cat galloped toward the door as it opened, yowling as if he were being chased by an army of slavering canines. The feline's headlong flight was accompanied by a prolonged shriek.

"Banshee Botox!" a woman caterwauled from deep inside the store. "Close the door! Don't let him out."

I quickly slammed the door behind me, cutting the agent behind me off in mid-stride.

A.P. yelped in pain from the wrong side of the entrance.

A woman came scurrying out of the stacks, rushing over to grab the cat, who was almost as big as a full-sized dachshund and sported only one and a half ears.

The feline's longish black fur was matted and sparse in spots, making him look like he'd spent the better part his life on the streets. White fur speckled the big cat's cheeks and chin, marking him as a feline of the older variety. His large, expressive eyes were a silvery-green and probably the most attractive thing about him.

Which wasn't saying much.

"Fenwald, you naughty boy," the woman said, her accent strident and British. "You're getting that bath whether you want it or not."

She looked at me through a pair of large tortoiseshell glasses, shoving them up a pug nose and peering at me as if I were a particularly nasty bug. "What is it, then? Do ya need a book?"

The door behind me opened, and A.P. came inside the store, rubbing his decidedly red nose. He glared at the woman behind the square glasses. "Alice. That cat is a menace."

I expected her to buckle under his severe disappointment. Instead, she grinned.

"Oy, Pudsy. How's things? You're looking a bit pinkish about the old snout there, eh?" Her laughter was a series of odd snorts that vibrated the glasses down her nose. She reached up and poked them back into place with a bandaged finger covered in black ink. "Ah," she said, her smallish brown eyes rolling back to me. "So, this is my new apprentice, then?" She looked me over with a critical eye. "She'll do." The woman offered me a work-roughened hand. "I'm Alice, Keeper of the Artifacts. You're Naida?"

I nodded, struck dumb by the reality in front of me. In my mind, I'd pictured a tall, powerful woman with a calm, no-nonsense manner as Keeper. My imagination might have even given her a long staff that shot electricity from the tip. Alice didn't fit that image in any respect.

Jerking her head toward the side, Alice said. "Come on, then. I'll make us a spot of tea." She carried the big cat with her as she slouched toward a nook across from the sales counter. The space sported a miniature stove, a tiny sink, and a short counter, which was covered in tea-making things and had a small refrigerator tucked beneath it. The oven door was open, and a comfortable warmth oozed from its interior. The cat immediately sprawled in front of it and began to bathe, clearly enjoying the heat.

With a jolt, I realized Alice was using the ancient appliance to warm the bookstore. "Is the heater broken?" I asked, pulling my coat closer as I shivered. I wasn't looking forward to spending a winter shivering and sniffling day and night.

Alice flipped a dismissive hand. "It's just having a fit. It'll be right as rain in no time."

I sent A.P. a worried glance, and he shook his head. "You need to get that fixed, Alice," he told the woman. "It was part of your apprenticeship agreement with the Société."

She ignored him completely, motioning negligently toward the small, three-person table in the center of the open space at the front of the store. A high, narrow window above the tea nook showed the clear blue of an early-January sky. The bright sunshine painted a golden ribbon across the bookstore's ratty carpet and bathed the round table in warmth. "Have a seat, Naida." She glanced at A.P. "You too, Pudsy. I'll have tea ready in two shakes."

I looked at A.P. and smiled, mouthing, "Pudsy?"

He shook his head dismissively.

While the tea steeped, Alice pulled the oven door wide. Grabbing a dingy towel that was appliqued with a large black cat which looked nothing like Fenwald, she tugged a flat pan from the oven's interior. She carefully extracted three pale, oblong biscuits from the pan, arranging them like spokes on a wheel in the center of a chipped white plate and sliding the rest back inside the oven.

Alice placed the snack on the table between us. "Scones. My specialty."

Having missed breakfast that morning, I smiled in anticipation. "Thank you. They smell delicious."

Alice gave me a pleased smile and returned to her tea prep.

Fenwald wandered over and sat down a few feet away from the table, staring at me through an unfathomable green gaze.

I reached for a scone, eyeing the dark spots marking its golden surface and wondering what they were. I hoped they weren't raisins. *Maybe blueberries?* I thought, hopefully.

A.P. reached out and touched my hand with a finger,

shaking his head and frowning as I lifted it toward my mouth.

Grinning, I took a bite.

"Ow!" I said before I could stop myself.

A.P. sat back and shook his head.

"Watch out, sweetums. They're hot."

I pulled the scone from my mouth and looked at the shallow dent my teeth had made in it. Feeling my front teeth to make sure they were still intact, I arched my brows at A.P.

He chuckled soundlessly. Reaching for another scone, he held it above the table for a moment, glancing over at Alice, he asked, "Is that a new thriller section, Alice?"

The Keeper lifted her head and looked into the bookstore. "Yes. Blimey, you do have a keen eye. I moved them from the back because I've seen new interest in thrillers of late." Alice wandered over to the books in question and ran her hand lovingly over their perfectly arranged spines.

While she was distracted. The Société agent slammed his scone against the edge of the table, coughing loudly to cover the noise, and broke a large chunk off the end of it. He threw the piece to Fenwald. It hit the carpet with the weight of a large marble and skittered to a spot a few inches from the cat.

Fenwald eyed the heavy offering and then lifted a derisive gaze to A.P., as if to say, *I'm not eating that.* Not wasting any time considering the offering, the big cat reached out with a large paw and whacked it away.

We watched it skitter beneath the cabinet where Alice kept her assortment of teas, out of sight.

I wondered how many other bits of bad baking the cat had "stored" beneath the cabinet. Then I decided I probably didn't want to know.

"I find I'm growing fond of the genre," Alice said, oblivious as she returned to her tea-making. She glanced over her shoulder at me. "How about you, Naida? What's your favorite genre?"

I flushed in embarrassment, not wanting to tell her in front of A.P. "Um, paranormal." It wasn't a lie...exactly...I did like some paranormal along with my romance.

Alice's grin widened. "A fine choice. I have a large selection in the store. Help yourself if you'd like. Just be sure to put a couple of dollars in the till for the rent."

My eyes went wide. "Rent?" There'd been no mention of rent. I'd thought I was going to be working off my room and board. It was an old-fashioned arrangement but a necessity. When my grandma had died a few months previous, she'd left me with a tiny house filled with ratty furnishings and a lot of debt that pretty much wiped out whatever I would earn from the sale of the house.

I had no money and no family that I knew of. If Agent A.P. hadn't come to me and told me there was an apprenticeship open for an artifact librarian, I'd have been in sad shape.

For once in my life, it had seemed like the winds of fate had blown in my favor. Though the Société agent had been vague about how he'd found me, murmuring something about being a friend of my grandma's.

I highly doubted that.

"Yes," said Alice. "I rent books for avid readers who don't have the space to store them all."

I nodded in understanding. "That makes sense."

She placed cups of tea in front of us and then pulled a third chair from the corner. Dropping into it with a sigh, Alice Parker fixed a speculative look on me. Then, lifting her teacup to her mouth, she said, "So, Naida Griffith, tell me why I should hire you as an apprentice for Keeper of the Artifacts?"

My mind went blank. I glanced toward A.P., but he wasn't paying attention to us. He'd pulled out his cell phone and seemed to be checking his emails.

I was on my own.

"Um…" I said stupidly. Stalling for time, I tucked a long strand of my curly brown hair behind one ear. Digging deep, I discarded options as quickly as they occurred to me. I couldn't tell her it was because I'd just turned twenty-two and needed a job. From what A.P. had told me, Keepers were born to wrangle artifacts. It wasn't a career choice. It was their legacy. I didn't want Alice to know I wasn't really suited for the job. She'd find out soon enough.

After a moment that stretched farther than the last pair of size eight jeans I'd tried to pull on over my size ten hips, I finally said the only thing that came to mind. "I get migraines, and strange objects seem to follow me around." I cringed inwardly. As random statements went, it was somewhere in the realm of "I see dead people."

To my shock, Alice cocked her head, narrowed her small eyes behind the massive glasses, and smiled. "Well now, that's just perfect. Okay then. Let's get started."

～

Read more Unbaked Croakies: https://books2read.com/unbaked

ALSO BY SAM CHEEVER

If you enjoyed **Croakies Dictum**, you might also enjoy these other fun mystery series by Sam. To find out more, visit the **BOOKS** page at www.samcheever.com:

Enchanting Inquiries Paranormal Mysteries - **For more fun adventures with Naida, Sebille, and Wicked!**

Reluctant Familiar Paranormal Mysteries

Yesterday's Paranormal Mysteries

Gainfully Employed Mysteries

Silver Hills Cozy Mysteries

Country Cousin Mysteries

And More...

ABOUT THE AUTHOR

USA Today and WSJ Bestselling Author Sam Cheever writes contemporary and paranormal mystery and suspense, creating stories that draw you in and keep you eagerly turning pages. Known for writing great characters, snappy dialogue, and unique and exhilarating stories, Sam is the award-winning author of 100+ books.

To learn more about Sam and her work, visit her at one of her online hotspots:
www.samcheever.com
samcheever@samcheever.com

www.ingramcontent.com/pod-product-compliance
Lightning Source LLC
Chambersburg PA
CBHW060546260626
47161CB00003B/1075